DEAD
WRONG

A gripping detective thriller full of suspense

HELEN H. DURRANT

Published 2016 by Joffe Books, London.

www.joffebooks.com

ISBN-13: 978-1523358601

Prologue

The torrent of kids crashed, pushed and clattered their way down the school staircase, and the air was filled with expletives.

"Ian! You stupid bastard!" Gavin Hurst wailed. "You'll cripple me with those bloody boots."

Ian Callum Edwards gave his friend a sharp shove as he bent down to rub his lower leg.

"There's the kid," he pointed gleefully, ignoring Gavin. "Let's have him."

The kid in question had stopped halfway up the stairs and was eyeing the pair with trepidation. Gavin Hurst and Ian were bad news, and he was the current object of their bullying attentions.

"Never mind the kid, what about my fucking ankles," Gavin protested, getting his own back by pushing Ian against the wall.

"Sod your feet; let's get the kid — have some fun." Ian glowered back. "For the last hour he's been sat in that classroom picking his fat nose — almost made me retch, filthy retard!"

David Morpeth clenched his fists together nervously and lumbered down the staircase towards them, his face red from the exertion.

"Too much for you, fat boy?" Gavin Hurst taunted, thrusting his face into the boy's as he tried to squeeze past.

"Where's your bodyguard today? Finally got tired of mollycoddling you?"

"Leave . . . me . . . alone." Morpeth's voice quivered, "Because if you don't, you'll be in big trouble."

"Sounds like fat boy's trying to scare us," Ian whooped at Gavin, while his mate blocked David's way. "Are you scared, Gav? Cos I'm not. I think we should teach this no-mark a lesson in manners — what d'you say?"

David lowered his head and closed his eyes. He was trying to think. His brother, Michael, had told him what to say to these two, but he'd forgotten.

"Do you like my new boots?" Ian demanded, lifting his knee and practically thrusting it in the boy's face. "Got 'em cheap. Cheap and *nasty*, that's my boots." He aimed a sharp kick at the boy, catching him in the shins.

David Morpeth screeched, shrinking back against the stair-rail.

"Not so brave now, are you, fat boy? Not without big brother to hold your hand."

Another kick, followed by a couple of slaps around the face.

"Pity we've got no more paint; could have done a proper job this time. Kelly's off, so no one here to clean you up. What do you say, fat boy, want to come to the caretaker's shed and we'll look for some? We can colour you a different shade this time — you'd look good in green." He laughed. "Green and sickly — what d'you say?"

David was shaking. He looked from one face to the other. Did they mean that? Would they really do all that again — cover him in all that awful paint?

"If you don't leave me alone I'll tell Sir," He'd finally remembered the sentence his older brother had rehearsed with him.

But the words didn't have the expected effect. The pair simply laughed out loud, and then they started to pull at the boy's clothing, loosening his shirt from the waistband of his pants and tearing at the buttons on his jacket.

"Which *Sir* would that be then? That stupid sod who calls himself the head?" Ian roared, shaking his head. "Bloody shower, the lot of them. Got no balls. Believe me, fat boy, they won't take us on, and especially not for your sake — loser!"

Ian grabbed hold of the boy's tie and tried to spin him around. David's eyes were glued to the floor as he tried to avoid the worst of those heavy boots. He was wheezing and his chest felt heavy. He was starting to get an asthma attack. He needed his inhaler, and quick.

He didn't have the breath to speak, or to shout, and he felt dizzy. His eyes searched around wildly, looking for help. But there was no one else around. The other kids gave the pair a wide berth. No one wanted to get mixed up in what went on in Ian and Gavin's version of the world. Better not to look.

Gavin pushed the boy to Ian, who spun him again and pushed him back. They were all three perched precariously on a couple of stairs. David Morpeth was clumsy by nature — this could only go on for a few minutes before he fell.

But David took a deep breath and tried to escape. He intended to hurry down the rest of the staircase and out of harm's way — but Gavin Hurst was too fast for him. He took hold of David's jacket and threw him towards Ian. But instead of taking hold of the boy, Ian stuck out a booted foot, kicked him in the backside and sent him hurtling down the remainder of the steps.

Chapter 1

He was cold, cold to the bone, and there was pain too. Sharp, stabbing pains shot up and down his arm, and yet his fingers were numb; the pain there was all switched off. He turned his head, just a little, and tried to focus his eyes. He had to make this stop — he had to sort out his hand.

He blinked; no way could this be happening. He was standing naked in what looked like a stone cellar. How had he got here? His mind was a blank; he racked his brain, but there was nothing. He was bound to something cold and hard against a stone wall. Pulling hard against whatever was holding him, he tried to yell out. That didn't work either; his mouth was stuffed with something that tasted foul.

He hung his head, almost resting his chin on his chest for a few seconds. He needed to work this out, but his head was spinning. Perhaps he was dreaming. Perhaps he'd taken some bad gear and was hallucinating? It happened to his best mate often enough. The stupid sod was always off his head, and now it was his turn. That must be it. He inhaled deeply, and turned to look again at the source of the pain. This time it was easier — this time he could see with perfect clarity. This was no dream.

He squinted in disbelief. This was a nightmare. All the fingers of his right hand were gone.

The movement distracted the man in white paper overalls and he looked up. The lad flinched with surprise as they locked eyes. Who was he and where had he come from? Why was he dressed like that and why was he doing this to him? The man was stood in the centre of the cellar and seemed to be reading a newspaper — the local rag? He was turning the pages in quick succession, getting progressively angrier each time. Why, what did he expect to see written there?

"There's nothing," the man shouted. "They're bloody useless — still no mention of either of you." He threw the paper to the floor in disgust, watching the greedy newsprint soak up the stale urine that had gathered in a foetid puddle under the young man's feet. "You know what this means?" he folded his arms. "It means that all this has been for nothing; and it'll stay that way unless I change tactics."

The man was a nutter, that was it, and a clever nutter too because it would take someone with unusual talent to corner him. He had to get out — and quick.

"Be still, maggot brain! I need to think," the man barked at the naked, struggling figure. "The press can't ignore this; I won't let them," he assured the lad. "And as for your families," he scoffed, "incredible as it seems, no one has missed you yet." He placed his hands on his hips and moved closer to his captive. "Sad, eh? Not even that thin-lipped, dyed blonde who calls herself your mother has bothered to come looking."

Who did this nutter think he was? This wasn't how folk behaved around him and he was becoming more and more angry. He wanted to roar a reply, to scream at him, to use his fists and beat this bastard into the ground. No one spoke to him like that, they wouldn't dare. But he couldn't — he was helpless.

"Surely someone out there must wonder what's happened to you," the voice taunted. "Doesn't anyone wonder why you're not lurking in the estate alleyways dealing dope anymore?

This was stupid — how had he got into this mess? The lad closed his eyes, he needed to think. He tried to reassure himself that it would be okay. But would it? Not if no one knew he was here it wouldn't.

"It wasn't supposed to be like this," his captor said softly. "You see I'd expected publicity, bags of it. I'd expected the local paper to be asking questions by now. People don't go missing every day, not even in this godforsaken community. So tell me, where the hell are the headlines, bad boy?"

The gag in his mouth meant he couldn't say anything so he simply gurgled a frustrated reply and pulled again on the ties.

"I've never done this sort of thing before," his captor confided, moving even closer to the lad. "So I'm bound to make mistakes. As far as killing goes, I'm a rank amateur. What d'you think? I'll just have to try harder, won't I?

The pain, the anger, and the tirade of words was all too much and he slipped into semi-consciousness again.

"I'd wake up if I were you," were the words that dragged him back. As the lad's head lolled forwards again, the man sneered, "Wake up, or you'll miss all the fun."

The young man was trying to stay conscious. For fuck's sake, he needed his wits about him, but the pain was excruciating.

"As it is, I've had to start without you."

More of the nutter's sniggering and he could feel the bastard's breath on his wounded hand.

"No matter — I haven't done the other one yet." And the snigger grew into a demonic chuckle.

The sound cut into the young man's very soul.

"I'm afraid it had to be done, and it's no more than you deserve. You and the others need to be punished."

Punished — was that what was going on? But for what and why like this? He'd never done anything like this to anyone, never even come close. Had he been able to, the youth would have made the bastard talk, but as it was, he was unlikely to ever know.

The lad was stood upright, tied to metal girders set against the wall, gagged and barely conscious. Another weak moan issued through the filthy gag stretched between his teeth. He tried to move his limbs against the harsh grip of the cable ties, but the movement caused them to bite deeper into his flesh, worsening the pain.

"I've come to the conclusion, maggot brain, that this situation calls for some upgrading," the voice droned on. "I need to do something that won't fail to get us talked about." The words were directed at the limp, shivering mass as if he expected a suggestion. "Keeping you here isn't enough."

The lad felt hot suddenly, a fever? His captor's voice sounded far away and was suddenly lighter. Had he realised this was all a big mistake? Would he let him go?

"Guess what? You caused so much trouble when you were free that no one wants you back. At least if they do, they're not telling the police, or anyone else for that matter."

The young man wanted to switch him off — he was like a persistent insect buzzing in his ear. Obviously he'd expected much more than this silence. He must have expected the folk of that damned estate to rise up and come looking for him. He'd obviously relied on there being press involvement. But all he'd got was a big fat nothing. If his situation hadn't been so horrific, he would have laughed in the fool's face.

He watched the man clad in white coveralls rub his head as if trying to encourage an idea, release a genie. He would be doubly dangerous now. He wanted results and was losing patience. The look, the body language, it was something the lad recognised. His captor was simmering, ready to blow. Seconds later these assumptions were confirmed as the man snatched up a hammer from the metal bench and slammed it down hard. It made a resounding crash, and the young man shrank in terror. Next time that might be his head.

Tied tight or not, he was shaking with fright, but the sharp clunk of steel on steel also served to clear his mind. He tried to mumble something, some words of appeal to this bastard's better nature, but the gag turned the words into muffled gibberish.

"No one's noticed he's disappeared yet either." The captor glanced at the bundle stashed in a corner of the cellar. "I can't wait forever for them to wake up to the fact that you're missing too."

So he'd got his mate as well. He tried to push the fabric from his mouth with his tongue and mumbled louder. He coughed. He hadn't had any food or drink for what seemed like days. His mouth was so dry that the gag stuck to his teeth, almost solid by now and rancid. He wanted to explain that of course he would be missed, his other mates and Kelly, they'd be worried about him.

"No one's bothered about either of you. Don't you find that rather sad?"

He was frantically trying to free himself now by pulling forward hard. His last hope was Kelly. He knew she'd be bothered. She always came looking for him when he disappeared. But would she be in time?

He was afraid, but that wasn't the only reason why he was shaking. He knew his body would by now be dealing with the heroin withdrawal. Why didn't this fucking bastard just let him go? None of this was his fault. Whatever he was supposed to have done, he certainly didn't deserve this.

The trembling had started and it would get worse. Normally nothing scared him, but now he was terrified. He didn't know how long he'd been here; he hadn't been conscious all the time, but he knew he wouldn't get out alive, not without a bloody miracle.

He watched as the man in the white coveralls studied an array of objects he had on his metal bench. The youth squinted — he could make out a whole lot of stuff on there: the contents of the average toolbox, plus a few things you'd use in the garden. With a little relief, he noted that there was no gun. Mind you, at least that would be quick.

His stomach somersaulted as the man picked up the heavy-duty secateurs and fondled them gently with his latex-gloved hands. They'd be sharp, the lad reasoned with a shudder. Had he used them to cut the fingers from his right hand? He watched as the man took a cloth and wiped the secateurs with meticulous care. Perhaps he had, and it looked very much like he was about to use them again.

"You'll be leaving me soon," were the next words the young man heard. And to accompany them the snap as the man used the secateurs to cut into a small piece of dowel. Obviously satisfied that they were up to the job, he advanced towards his captive.

"I'm not going to pretend, this is going to hurt. But I need your fingers for my little plan. You do want to be free of this place, and from me, don't you?"

Yes, but not this way. The lad shook his head, he was frantic. He thrashed about as much as he could in an effort to struggle free. He made a weak fist with his good hand, pulling hard against the girders. He could only shriek through the gag, as the ties embedded themselves deeper into his thin arms. He felt the warm blood trickle over his wrists and knew it was useless.

He couldn't see properly in the gloom. He couldn't scream and struggling was too hard and painful. Suddenly he retched, feeling the bitter vomit escape around the gag before dripping slowly down his body. He felt the warm flow of the vile-smelling fluid trickle over his belly, and he knew he would die here, naked, cold, and filthy.

"Relax your hand," the man said soothingly as he approached, wrinkling his nose in distaste at the smell. "That looks painful . . ." He looked down at the jagged remnants of bone protruding from the boy's right hand, and the way the blood ran in rivulets to join the other fluids on the floor.

"Let me see . . ." His grip was firm, as he pondered the anatomy. "I've never really looked properly before, but the human hand is really quite fascinating." Letting it drop, he took hold of the other hand. Giving his captive a comforting smile, he separated out the index finger, wielded the secateurs with practised confidence and cut just below the knuckle joint.

"One for sorrow . . ." He frowned in concentration.

The pain was unbearable. The lad tried to scream but the noise that emanated from behind the gag was more like the howl of some wild creature than a sound made by a man. His tortured body jerked uncontrollably, he was losing it. Finally shock thrust him back into a welcome blackness.

* * *

Satisfied with his efforts, the man in the white overalls produced a cell phone. Concentrating in the dim light, he found the video function and, returning to his unconscious captive, pointed the camera at the bloodied hand.

"Not sure what I'll do with this," he muttered to himself, shrugging. "But what I do know is it'll get me publicity. Who knows, by tonight you might be an internet sensation," he said, slapping the boy's face. "Shame you'll not be around to bask in your fame."

Taking the secateurs again in one hand, and holding the mobile in the other, he detached the middle finger.

"Two for joy." He smiled. "Not very joyful now though, are you, you little fool?"

There was no sound this time; the youth was unconscious. The man deftly removed the remaining fingers, continuing to intone the rhyme and film this brutal little interlude. He recorded the whole sequence, from the first agonising cut to the way they plopped one by one onto the urine-puddled floor, like anaemic chipolatas.

He got out the plastic carrier bag from a drawer under the table. The special one he'd put by for this very purpose. He gathered up the fingers, shook off the fluid, and dropped them in. He tied a knot and threw the bag onto his bench. As he did so, his attention was caught by the other bag, the one containing the money he'd found on the lad when he took him. He hadn't reckoned on there being so much. Drug dealing was obviously a lucrative business. The money was a problem he didn't have a solution for just yet. But he'd work on it. Something was bound to occur to him.

It wouldn't be right to leave him like this. The tiny stubs of what was left of his fingers were bleeding profusely. He really should put the young man out of his misery. It would be the kindest thing to do.

He picked up a knife, long and sharp. Would it cut through bone? He really didn't fancy sawing away at a limb until it slowly surrendered to the thin steel of a blade. He picked up an axe, studying it thoughtfully. He used it for chopping wood. He always kept his tools in good condition and, like the secateurs, it was sharp, and it was a good weight to handle. He ran an exploratory finger along its edge. Would this do? Would this cut through bone or just splinter it? He knew precious little about human anatomy, but one thing he did know — there would be blood. A lot.

His avid daily reading of the press, looking for news of the disappearances, had resulted in a large pile of newspapers. He gathered them up and spread them around the floor under the lad's feet. They would serve to soak up some of the blood and make his clean-up task easier.

If he'd had more storage room, then he could have despatched him differently, but he needed to squeeze this body into the freezer along with the other one — once he'd dealt with him. So he had no choice. Both bodies would be cut into smaller, more manageable parts.

He was sure now that he'd done the right thing. He was confident that by the start of the new week everyone would know about him. At long last he'd be headline news. An excited shiver fluttered down his spine and a self-satisfied smile passed across his face. He would use the axe.

Giving the implement a few practice swings, he walked towards the young man. The little maggot was groaning now as consciousness seeped back. He had heard the footsteps and was pulling against his restraints. His tormentor had to admire the boy's strength. It probably came from some primal sense of preservation, urging him to fight one last time. His smile was grim.

"Careful, lad, you must be in pain."

The young man smelled vile. The vomit was still dripping off his chest. He was bleeding heavily and was stood in his own urine and waste. What he was about to do would put him out of all this misery.

Raising the axe high above his head, he swung hard with confidence. Ignoring the splatter of blood and the thud of steel on flesh, he heard the reassuring clang as the axe met the rusty cast-iron girder behind the left knee cap. Happy with this outcome, he swung again, above the right knee.

He stood back and watched the blood pour onto the floor. He watched the lad's body twitch with shock and pain. He watched until the body moved no more, feeling intensely pleased with his handiwork.

He wanted a photograph, he wanted to capture the peculiar way the youth's detached legs, still bound at the ankles, leant away from his torso. He fumbled in his pocket for the phone, feeling an unfamiliar thrill fizz like electricity through his body.

This was a feeling he could get used to.

Chapter 2

Monday

Tom Calladine could think of better ways of spending a Monday morning, but the pain had kept him awake most of the night, so he had no choice but to bite the bullet. Moving his hand up to his jaw, he tried to rub the offending area, but the dentist moved it away, tut-tutting in his ear.

"Just a few more seconds, Inspector, then it'll all be over," he assured him, giving a final prod to his handiwork. "There, all done." The dentist passed him a hand mirror. "Have a look, good as new." There was pride in his voice.

Tom Calladine rubbed his jaw again and winced. He didn't care what it looked like, just so long as it didn't ache any more.

"It should settle down quite quickly now." The dentist smiled reassuringly as he removed his gloves and rinsed his hands in the sink. "But if the pain does get too much, then take a couple of Paracetamol. You won't need anything stronger."

Calladine hoped he was right. Over an hour in the chair, his mouth held open with some sort of metal scaffolding, was all he was prepared to put up with for one day. He hated dentists: the surgery, the instruments, and the knowledge that what lay ahead would hurt. Root canal treatment was particularly grim.

"I'll see you in six months, Inspector. Don't leave any more problems until they're as bad as this though," he warned, nodding at Calladine's mouth. "At your age you should really make an effort to look after your teeth. I know how busy you are, but your teeth are important, Tom."

Yet another reference to his age, Calladine thought with annoyance. So he'd turned fifty, what of it? Did that mean his body was about to give up the ghost and all his teeth fall out? He was getting a little tired of all the remarks he kept getting from people who should know better. They ought to know that with his level of fitness there was still plenty of life and work left in him yet.

Calladine mumbled something humourless and, rising from the chair, he turned his mobile back on. He didn't want to talk age, or even worse, shop. He just wanted to regain the feeling in his mouth and be able to down a cup of strong tea. He was relieved when, almost at once, his phone rang. Casting an apologetic glance at the dentist, he answered it.

A female voice spoke, "We've got a gruesome one on the Hobfield."

It was his sergeant, Ruth Bayliss. She was a woman not given to exaggeration, so if she said gruesome then that's what it was.

"A jogger and his dog found some severed fingers in a carrier bag on the common earlier this morning."

There was silence as Calladine took this in. "Not an accident, I take it," he mumbled. His mouth was still numb.

"I'd say not, boss. According to Doc Hoyle the fingers were crudely removed and the bag was left on the seat of a kid's swing," she told him. "Just plonked there, deliberately, for anyone to find."

"You're talking about the play area at the edge of the common?"

"Yep, the one close to Leesdon Centre," she confirmed. "Just as well it was found early. There's a playgroup nearby, and they use it regularly. Can you imagine if a kid had found it?"

So — it was over. The long, uneventful summer had finally ended. A shocking end, but at least it felt more 'normal' than the strange limbo the nick had been in these last months. The case might be gruesome alright, but he still felt the familiar excitement thread down his spine.

It had been so quiet that they'd started taking bets at the station on how long it would be before the Hobfield Estate erupted again. There'd been no trouble for weeks. No beatings, very few arrests, and they were all twitchy. His work this summer had been so quiet, so dull, he'd almost sleep-walked through it.

Nonetheless, the images this news conjured in his mind made his flesh creep. Was this the work of some nutter on the prowl? The next mad craze to hit the estate? He was used to the brutality; it was normal for that hell hole. It came with the gang culture and the drug dealing. But this? Even for the Hobfield this was excessive, to say the least. It smacked of something different. Extreme.

But hadn't the shooting in the spring been extreme too? God help them if this had anything to do with that.

Calladine had been trying to keep order on the Hobfield for most of his working life. It was a poisonous place, full of kids with no ambition and precious few prospects. He dreaded the day when one of them would rise up and shake a serious fist at the police. He dreaded the rise of some real hard case, some radical new gang leader who'd flout all the unwritten rules by which they operated. Not that there were many to flout.

He couldn't think who that might be. He knew most of the usual troublemakers. Was this someone new, reaching for the crown?

His sergeant voiced his thoughts, "Could be linked to the shooting." She was well aware that this would be uppermost on his mind. "If it is, then it could give us a break. Heaven knows, we need it."

"Not this sort of break, we don't." Had he sounded too abrupt? "It's too soon to jump to conclusions, Ruth. It could be anything. But if it is connected, some sort of retribution, then it could blow the case wide open . . . But then again, if it's not?" In the ensuing silence a shudder slid down his spine. Neither option was good. Retribution meant that someone on the Hobfield was one step ahead of him. On the other hand, a takeover or a war over territory were equally as bad. Both had the possibility to escalate beyond what the local police could deal with.

"We need to get this wrapped up, and quick. It will ripple through the gangs and give them no end of ideas if we don't sort it fast."

"It's possible that whoever carried out this latest atrocity has just found out who's responsible for that boy's death and decided to sort it himself," Ruth said.

Calladine wasn't surprised that Ruth had considered this; she was a good detective. But it didn't make him like the idea any better. If one of the scroats on the estate had cracked the case, then why hadn't he?

It had been a while since the kid had been killed and the trail had gone cold. He'd been shot dead one dark night, his young life snuffed out by a single bullet at close range. Surprisingly, there had only ever been a small amount of gun crime on the estate, so this had made everyone jittery. With most of the summer to mull it over, the police had it down as a takeover gone wrong.

Calladine didn't believe it. The kid was not a gang member for a start. The entire thing bothered him. It had been too clean; there was no evidence, nothing left at the scene. Was that just pure luck for whoever had carried out the murder, or was it something more sinister?

Unusually for the Hobfield, the victim, Richard Pope, had seemed like a good kid, so why had someone wanted him dead? The questions wouldn't go away. Why had he been a target? He had a fairly innocuous background, he didn't get into too much trouble — he just didn't stand out. Calladine could think of far worthier candidates for murder.

It galled him that, weeks down the line, they were no nearer to finding a solution. No one had seen anything, of course, and no one could offer anything helpful about the dead kid either. The team had put everything they had into the investigation and, six months later, they still had a big fat nothing. No witnesses and no forensics (apart from the bullet). Their failure depressed and annoyed Calladine.

As for the Hobfield Estate, it was weird, but there had been a kind of unholy peace among the different factions all summer. It hadn't felt right.

He had to find out what was going on and fast. Ruth's suggestion that someone had achieved what he hadn't been able to, and had now exacted revenge, made him shudder.

"OK, Ruth, I'm not far away. Where are you now?"

"I'm on the edge of the common, just off the Circle Road, sir. I've got the area cordoned off but I'm trying not to attract too much attention. With luck any onlookers will shrug it off as just another burnt-out car." She gave a sardonic laugh. "Doc Hoyle has been and gone. He's taken the bag and fingers to the mortuary. I've told Julian, so forensics will be examining the bag."

DS Ruth Bayliss walked away from the rest of the group. "SOCO are combing through everything, doing a fingertip search of the immediate area and I've got Dodgy knocking on doors along Circle Road." 'Dodgy' was Detective Constable Michael Dodgson, the latest recruit to the team. "I got here before anything was touched," she told Calladine. "The bag was just lying there, on the swing. Whoever left it, sure as hell wanted it found — and talked about."

"We have to stop that, for now at least. Have a word with the jogger. I don't want the press to get wind of this."

"Already sorted, sir. Turns out he's a solicitor, so he understands why he should keep his mouth shut."

"Get his statement. Did he see anything, anyone else hanging around?"

"He says not, but he did see the seven fifteen to Manchester pass along the road, and it was packed. Someone on that bus might have seen them. Should we think about putting something out, an appeal? No need to give the details."

Calladine wasn't keen. Until he knew where this was going, he didn't want the press involved.

"Not yet. You've got things sorted, well done. Check if there's any CCTV, particularly along the row of shops at the top end, then meet me at the mortuary and we'll see what Doc Hoyle has to say."

He sighed. The prospect of a case, after the long summer hiatus might be exciting, but someone seeking retribution for murder, or a possible new drugs war on the Hobfield didn't fill him with much joy either. The Hobfield was a cesspit, the embodiment of all that was wrong with the entire area. It was no place to conduct a satisfactory investigation.

* * *

The sign on the road that indicated entry to Leesdon said *Leesdon Village*, but *village* was a bit of a misnomer. The place was much too spread out and built up to deserve that particular description.

Calladine had watched Leesdon grow, seen it thrive briefly during the seventies and then take a spectacular nosedive after the Hobfield was built.

Ever since the mid-eighties, the area had gone steadily downhill. Calladine thought this was a great shame, because it was situated right in the middle of some fantastic countryside.

This was where Calladine had spent his life. He'd been born and raised in Leesdon and now lived in a small cottage just off the High Street.

Leesdon was one of a number of villages which were known collectively as Leesworth, situated in the Pennine foothills and steeped in industrial history. Quaint stone cottages bordered the village roads. The old stone woollen mills, once the main source of employment, had long since been converted into pricy apartments. This had brought in the business types, those hard-working souls who were happy to commute into Manchester every day and were prepared to pay through the nose for a pocket handkerchief of a flat.

But there had been no gentrification in Leesdon. Leesdon was the exception.

Once the Hobfield Estate had been established, no further development took place. The village was condemned to be the eternal poor relation of an otherwise desirable, upmarket area. News of the Hobfield's dubious reputation had spread, and the developers stayed away.

There weren't many amenities or quite enough shops; none of the big chains were here, and there hadn't been a bank for two decades, since some fool had tried robbing it.

But Leesworth Police Station remained; his own nick and the place in which he intended to work out the rest of his time with the force. And, of course, there was the hospital which served the local area and beyond. He was headed there now.

The *Cottage Hospital*, as it was still fondly called, had a small emergency department, several wards, and a mortuary.

Hopefully Hoyle would give him something he could use. There'd been nothing after the shooting, and Calladine knew the man well enough to know he felt this failure as acutely as Calladine himself.

You might say that Doctor Sebastian Hoyle was every bit as old school as he was. The doctor could easily have moved up the career ladder by transferring to one of the bigger acute hospitals within the Greater Manchester area, but he hadn't. Like Calladine, he remained firmly rooted in Leesdon. This gave the two men a common bond.

As he pulled in, Calladine could see Sergeant Ruth Bayliss pacing up and down the car park, talking into her mobile phone while she waited for him. She was wrapped up against the cold weather in a long woollen coat and scarf. Neither of these did her any favours on the appearance front. Ruth didn't follow fashion — she wore what she was comfortable in. She covered up mostly — those who knew her well knew that Ruth had a thing about her weight, and this coloured how she saw herself. But the truth was, it was all there. A different hairstyle, a little makeup and she could be a stunner. Ruth had small features and a clear, pale complexion. Lose the weight and change her attitude and she could give any female you mentioned a run for their money.

Calladine parked his small saloon car and nodded back as she greeted him with a wave. She'd worked as his sergeant for a number of years, and they got on well. Ruth could be highly critical of both his ideas and methods at times, but he knew that she considered him good at what he did. She could hardly think anything else — his team had the best clear-up rate in the nick.

And he was easy on the eye, even if he thought so himself. Not that he was vain but according to his mother, who was his greatest fan, he had lean angular good looks which suited his dark hair. In his younger days she'd likened him to some film star or other, which had caused far too much hilarity among his friends for comfort. He smiled to himself. Did she still think that, he wondered, now that his once mid-length dark hair was close cropped and fast turning to grey? She didn't say much that made any sense these days.

The regard was mutual. Calladine enjoyed working with Ruth, who was easy to get on with and good at her job. He trusted her. She was a very practical woman, and a real asset to his team. Apart from working together they also had friends in common. She'd been married briefly to the brother of his on-off girlfriend Monika. Combined with her plain speaking, this gave Ruth an edge with the inspector that the others didn't have. She often advised him, and pulled no punches. Calladine was hopeless where the women in his life were concerned, a failing he was well aware of, and he often turned to Ruth for help.

Despite this, Calladine knew precious little about Ruth's private life. If she were anything like him, he thought, she'd be damn lucky if she had one. But that didn't stop him wondering how she'd managed to get to her mid-thirties with no ties. She was probably too intelligent for most men — she saw straight through people, right to their flaws.

"Julian says he's got something for us already," she told him with a smile as he approached. "Says he can give us something really useful on the plastic bag when we get back."

Calladine nodded, thrusting his hands deep into his coat pockets against the icy wind. Once summer was done with, the cold seemed to set in hard around here. He shivered and felt his cheek twinge. He had questions, plenty of them, but his mouth was still numb and he couldn't trust his lips or tongue to work quite properly yet.

"You haven't forgotten, have you?" Ruth asked. "Monika's birthday; you said to remind you."

Calladine swore under his breath. He hadn't exactly forgotten, but he hadn't come up with any ideas either.

"Flowers?" he mumbled.

"You should try to do a little better than that, sir. You are trying to make this work — again." She raised her eyebrows. "Think of something she likes, something she's into."

Calladine knew that there were times when Ruth despaired of him — she thought Monika was a great idea. Monika didn't ask for much either, so the least he could do was give her something she'd appreciate for her birthday.

Calladine shrugged. "What d'you mean? As far as I can tell Monika's into her work — just like me." Monika was the manageress of the care home his mother lived in. When she was off-duty, she usually lay exhausted on the sofa in her flat. On the rare occasions when they were both free at the same time they went out for a meal or film. This was probably the reason their relationship was so shaky.

"Look, Tom, it's about time you made a decision. Are you serious about making this work? What you're doing is playing around with Monika's feelings and it isn't fair. It's a simple enough question — do you want her or don't you?"

The truth was, he didn't know. Ruth seemed to think Monika was right for him, so why the doubt? And having to decide on a present would bug him all day; he was no good at this sort of thing. Why did it have to be so damned difficult? She was a woman, wasn't she? So what the hell was wrong with flowers — surely a big bunch of them couldn't be wrong?

"Don't get flowers; get her something a little more personal, jewellery perhaps." They were by this time pacing along a hospital corridor. "What does she like?"

"She likes that blue stuff."

"Sapphires?" Ruth asked hopefully

"No, that bluey-green stuff — chunky little rock things."

"Jade?"

"No — turquoise, yes that's it, turquoise." He was pleased with himself for remembering. "I'll pop in to the jewellers, that little one in town, on my way home."

"You might be better off in the Antiques Centre; you know the one, off the bypass. I've seen some nice vintage jewellery in there."

That wasn't a bad idea; it was on his way home, provided he left early enough to catch it open.

"And sort your head out will you? All this indecision isn't good. Monika and you — you're good together." This was accompanied by a jab in the ribs.

But was *good together* enough? Shouldn't there be something more — a spark of excitement at least?

"Get your tooth sorted, did you?" She smiled, looking at his swollen lip. "I've got some painkillers back at the nick if you need them."

They had reached the mortuary and the conversation moved on to more professional matters.

"What's this all about, Ruth? Is it punishment, revenge, or our worst nightmare?" He rubbed at his cheek, trying to get rid of the numbness.

"It's different, that's for sure. We've seen plenty of beatings, loads of broken bodies lying black and blue in hospital, but nothing like this."

So, something new then — or someone. The nightmare prospect of an escalating turf war on the Hobfield lurked constantly, like a phantom, at the back of his mind. It troubled him whenever something happened that he couldn't explain — like now. If one of the hooligans decided to give it a real go, then guns were easy enough to get hold of, as the shooting had proved. They were only a few miles away from Manchester.

The drugs on the Hobfield were mostly supplied to the dealers by one man, Ray Fallon. *Fallon*. The mere thought of that name made Calladine cringe. The team from Manchester Central was keeping an eye on him, but had something gone wrong? Was Fallon slipping? Had the field somehow been left open?

"I have a bad feeling." He shivered. "Most of what happens between the gangs is a sudden flare-up, the result of an argument or a stand-off about territory. The gangs fight and they react. They don't chop off fingers. This doesn't feel like an internal war or an exasperated Fallon teaching some cocky bastard a lesson in manners either. Fallon would just have one of his minions use a baseball bat on the culprit. And if he had someone killed, we'd never find the body."

Ruth shot him a look. He could be right; this was more likely to be drugs-related than anything else. That was the nature of the Hobfield.

"Knowing who the fingers belong to will be a start."

Calladine nodded. "Or belonged to, Ruth." They stood at the mortuary door. "But we'll check with the ED while we're here. See if anyone's come in. I hope I'm wrong, but the owner, whoever the poor bastard is or was, is probably dead."

Silently, Calladine recited an endless list of names. But his gut instinct told him that it wouldn't end with the fingers. Once word got out, the dealers would want retribution — from each other. And from Fallon.

"Ah, Tom and Sergeant Bayliss," Hoyle greeted them as they entered the mortuary. He gestured towards the digits lined up on the table in front of them.

The scene was as odd as it was macabre. Calladine was more used to seeing an entire corpse laid out. The sight of these detached fingers, as well as thoughts about how they got that way, made him shudder.

"I was actually beginning to miss your company these last weeks." He nodded. "Yes, a quiet summer. Wondered where it would end . . . Spent most of mine working on a research paper. I'll let you read it sometime; it should interest you, Tom. It's all about getting an accurate time of death from studying foreign bacteria on the body. You know — whatever's left by flies, bugs, and the like."

"You should take up golf or something, Doc. Or come and have a few pints with the lads. You know — lighten up a bit."

Hoyle laughed and shook his balding head at the irony of that advice coming from the workaholic detective.

"Julian took the bag. That should provide some good evidence," Hoyle told him. "It was a plastic carrier from a supermarket and there was a receipt inside it. Julian will liaise with your lot back at the station. You should have no trouble tracing it. He'll also see if he can lift prints from the bag."

It was a reasonable start, careless on the part of the perpetrator, which was good for them.

"Male. Quite decayed." They were looking at the fingers. "But not overly so. They haven't been hanging about too long. See," he pointed to the finger tips with a pencil, "they've just started to blacken. But I'll know more once I've done the tests. If there's anything in the database then DNA will tell you who we've got."

"Prints?"

"Bit ambitious that, Tom, but I might manage a partial."

"I could do with that particular result asap, Doc, if I'm to find out who this is. That and the DNA is about all I've got to go on."

"Oh, I think you've got a little more than that, Tom. Look." He pointed to faint marks just above the knuckle on some of the fingers. "Tattoos I think."

"Can you decipher them?"

"You know me; I'll do my best." The doctor smiled.

"Anything you can get, Doc. I need to find out who this poor sod is — or was — as quickly as I can."

"Poor sods, Tom," Hoyle corrected him. "The digits are not all from the same individual."

"Are you sure?" Surprised, Calladine bent to take a closer look at the grisly remnants.

"Count them," Hoyle nodded. "There are three thumbs and nine fingers." The pathologist shrugged. "In my book that means you're looking for at least two victims."

Chapter 3

"I want the team in the main office for a meeting in five minutes."

Calladine took off his overcoat and threw it over the back of the chair in his office. He rummaged in his desk drawer for a few moments and pulled out a file labelled *Shooting*.

There wasn't much: the victim's name, Richard Pope, and some family details. He'd been the only child of older parents and had kept his nose clean. There was no police record, not even a caution. Not the type, then, to go get himself shot. He'd been just a face in the crowd — so why?

Calladine rubbed his sore cheek. All these months later, and they still didn't even know who his friends were, who he talked to — if anyone. They'd asked, but no one had come forward. Calladine didn't think he'd belonged to one of the gangs, but perhaps he'd been wrong to assume that.

For as long as he could remember Calladine had dreaded waking up one morning to find that there was a turf war raging on the Estate. Was this fingers incident the start of such a nightmare? If it was, then where did the shooting fit in — if it fitted at all?

Whatever the answer, there was a definite frisson of excitement among his colleagues as he strode into the main office. Ruth had already prepared the incident board. Images of those damned fingers, pictures of the receipt, scanned and emailed through from Julian, and the bag they'd been found in, were already posted up. All of it a gruesome and sobering reminder of what they were up against.

He stood before his assembled team.

"I know what you're all thinking," began Calladine, "but I want to say straight off that we don't have anything to link this to the shooting — or anything else." They were all watching him from their desks, their eyes glued to the scant evidence pinned to the board. Besides Ruth Bayliss, there were a detective sergeant, three detective constables — Simon Rockliffe (Rocco to his mates), Michael Dodgson (now known by all as 'Dodgy'), Imogen Goode, and Joyce, the admin assistant.

"As things stand, this could be anything." He pointed to the images on the board. "And that includes the start of a turf war."

He paused, stuffing his hands in his trouser pockets.

He had their complete attention. The entire nick had taken the lack of progress on the shooting as a personal failing. It wasn't true, of course. You couldn't build a case out of nothing.

"This morning, a number of human fingers were found in a plastic carrier bag in the play area of the common. Subject to DNA testing to confirm, we have two victims, but we don't have all the fingers." He cleared his throat. "It goes without saying that we need to know who the victims were — and fast. I say 'were' because I'm presuming, until we know different, that this is murder.

Given that they were found on the Hobfield, you probably think that the motive for this is drugs-related, but that's just an assumption and could be entirely wrong. You all know how the gangs operate — except perhaps

Dodgy." Calladine nodded at the new man. "They fight, with fists, bats, even knives, but up until this point we've had nothing like this."

The team was silent, almost visibly wondering, trying to calculate. What had they got? What were they looking at?

"Once we have the forensic results, we should have a couple of names. What we want for now is eyes and ears on the streets. Someone on the Hobfield will know something, at the very least be suspicious. Go through everything: CCTV . . ." Calladine turned to Rocco. "Have you brought in all the tapes?"

Rocco nodded his dark head. "The ones I could get. The off license and the newsagents do the surveillance properly. The others . . ." He shrugged. "The cameras are just a sham, only there to act as a deterrent."

"It all needs sifting through," Calladine told them. "I want to know who passed that way. We can only guess at the time scale. That play area is used at night by the older kids; you can tell by the broken beer bottles on the ground."

Rocco gave another nod. "We'll give it a thorough looking at, sir, don't worry."

He'd do a decent job. Rocco was a good detective and had a promising future ahead of him. He was tall and pleasant looking, with the kind of 'modern' looks that young women seemed to go for.

Calladine addressed the newest member of his team. "Dodgy, you've been knocking on doors. Anyone see anything?"

The young detective shook his head and bit nervously at his bottom lip. This was his first big case, and he probably wanted to please. He had a lot to live up to.

"It's alright, son." Calladine saw the worried look, and was sympathetic. The lad was still green — still trying to fit in. "Folk on that estate aren't keen to speak to the police;

they know it's a dangerous pastime to be seen squealing. But we're always hopeful, so it's worth a try."

"No one turned up at the emergency department," Ruth told them. "Despite what we've got, we can't presume the victims are dead, but with injuries like this they'll be in a pretty bad way if they're not. It's worth checking on the chemists in Leesdon, and then the ones in the wider area. See if anyone has asked for advice or bought a lot of first-aid stuff in the last few days."

Calladine looked at the board and scratched his head. "Where's Julian? I thought he had something on the bag—"

"I do." The man who walked into the room was tall, and walked with a slight swagger. He'd come straight from the lab at the hospital, and was still wearing a white coat, clutching a clipboard with a bundle of notes stuck to it.

"There's good news and bad, I'm afraid," he began. "We're lucky, Inspector. The receipt was issued by a supermarket that operates one of those loyalty schemes, so it has a membership number on it." This pronouncement was accompanied by a wave of his hand.

He paused — he was obviously enjoying the drama — then he coughed, taking up his position in front of the board. He was as tall as Calladine but Julian Batho was slight and wiry, whereas Calladine was broad-chested and well-built.

"It was issued to a Mrs Masheda. The shop gave me her address and, as I'm sure you know," he addressed the team, "she lives on the Hobfield."

Calladine's mouth pulled into a thin line. "Our call, I think, Julian." He removed the report from the forensic scientist.

"It was nothing of a job, Inspector. It took all of two minutes to establish the name."

Calladine didn't like it when Julian did this sort of thing. He was a forensic scientist, not a detective, and he could have missed something.

"You know the name, Tom?" Julian pushed.

Indeed he did. Masheda was a name he knew only too well. He nodded at Ruth. "Anything else we should know, Julian?"

Julian Batho stood for a few moments basking in the admiration of Imogen Goode, and then he winked at her. The detective constable wriggled on her seat, smiled, and then adjusted her dark-framed glasses nervously.

She was flirting with him, Calladine realised, watching the pair of them. He knew Ruth had been observing these two over the past few weeks. Perhaps she was right, and despite Imogen's protestations to the contrary, something was going on between them. He could understand it in a way. Julian was a serious, nerdy sort, and Imogen was a complete computer geek, but that was as far as it went, because physically they were ill matched. Poor Julian was tall and gangly with large facial features, whereas Imogen was quite a stunner. Ruth had told him, that in her opinion, this situation was bound to end badly. And she could be right, because as far as Calladine could remember, romances within the team had never worked out well.

"What would you like, Inspector?" Julian whispered conspiratorially in Calladine's ear — playing to the room. "What can science add to the mix that plain old detection can't?"

Tom didn't have time for the scientist's odd sense of humour, or his beliefs that science alone could solve a case. He gave him a look that said so, clearly. Forensic science was important, vital if they were to get the right outcome in court. But if forensic evidence was all they had to go on, then half the cases would have stayed unsolved. Calladine trusted his instincts. He had a sort of sixth sense, or perhaps it was something that had developed over the years with experience. But to date it had never let him down. "Do you have anything else or not?" he demanded tersely, knitting his brows.

"Well, I have a name." Julian Batho announced this proudly, and almost took a small bow as a buzz of response flew around the team. "Ian Callum Edwards."

"Ice."

Calladine's response was almost immediate.

The buzz got louder. They all recognised the name, and knew the young man it belonged to. All, that was, except Dodgy.

"Ice?" He turned to Imogen beside him.

"A well-known young thug and drug dealer. Ice is his nickname," she explained. "You see the word written all over the estate — you know, graffiti. It's written in great big bubble letters and painted blue. It's his tag."

"We got a match on his DNA almost immediately," Julian told the team. "Once Doctor Hoyle took a closer look, we could also see what the tattoos on his fingers spelled out — his initials."

Calladine gestured for the team to be quiet, as Julian continued.

"Then there was this." He handed Calladine a photo. "This is an image of what we found on the receipt, and it's got nothing to do with the supermarket. Our man is leaving us his mark, a tag of his own. His signature."

Calladine felt the hairs on the back of his neck prickle. He didn't like this. Those instincts were at it again. They were warning him that this case would turn out to be something big, and very unpleasant.

The mark was a miniature imprint of a bloodied hand made by some sort of stamp that had been inked — in this case with bright red ink. A bag of severed fingers, a bloodied hand; the message was plain enough. And it was nothing like anything he'd seen before on the Hobfield.

Calladine felt his stomach heave and he almost gagged. This wasn't Fallon; this wasn't how that particular gangster operated. Fallon wouldn't leave a mysterious mark to puzzle the police, or anyone else. Fallon's style was a good kicking, enough to put the boy in hospital for a few days, then tell everyone about it.

Why the gang graffiti, what did it mean? This was a tag he hadn't seen before — if that's what it was. Was this a show by some new thugs on the block? It certainly seemed that way at first. A takeover. Or was that what they were supposed to think? Were they supposed to believe that someone tougher, smarter, had come along, and this was the new method of punishment?

"I've seen this somewhere," Rocco said, as the photo of the bloodied hand was passed around. "I'll have to check it out, but I'm sure it's daubed on the gable end of the off licence on Circle Road."

"Gang tags are serious business," Imogen explained to Dodgy. "They send out a message to rivals, the law and anyone else who fancies their chances. It's like a code saying 'keep off, this is our territory.'"

Tag aside, they now had a name, and a link to the crime. All very neat, but perhaps a little too neat. And that was exactly like Fallon; putting someone else in the frame was a favourite ploy of his. The DI's head was full of conflicting ideas.

He had that feeling again. It wasn't rational, given what little they knew, but he had the feeling that this latest atrocity was being flaunted in their faces. That the perpetrator was playing some sort of *catch me if you can* game with them.

"Okay, this changes things. We need to know when Edwards was last seen. Ruth and I will go to the Hobfield and visit his mother. We'll tell her the bad news and appoint a liaison officer to stay with her. We don't want any of this getting out, not yet. I don't want Donna Edwards, or any of you talking to the press. We'll deal with them as and when we have to."

The team was mostly in agreement, but Ruth did wonder if, on this occasion, having some publicity might help.

"He has a girlfriend — Kelly Griggs," Calladine continued. "She and Edwards have an infant son, and she's got a flat in Fieldfare House, the smaller of the tower blocks. We'll visit her too. I want to know the last time she saw him. Don't mention the find to her, not yet, not until we know what we're dealing with."

He transferred his gaze to Rocco. "You and Dodgy visit the Masheda family." This was said with a grim edge to his voice. "Young Malcolm in particular. As I recall there's not a lot of love lost between him and Ice, not since Kelly."

He thought for a moment and then looked at Imogen, who was making notes. "I'm afraid that leaves the CCTV," he apologised, knowing that this would mean hours of watching endless tapes. "See what you can do with it." He smiled. "Also do as Ruth suggested, give the chemists in Leesdon and town a ring. See if anyone's been in asking for advice or bought large amounts of dressings in the last few days."

It was a long shot, but they couldn't treat this as anything but a serious assault until they found Ian Edwards, dead or alive.

"Right, folks!" He raised his voice above the chatter. "Back here at five for an update. Okay?"

* * *

"How d'you all cope?" Detective Sergeant Don Thorpe asked Ruth, as the team meeting broke up.

He was a sergeant on the station's other team of detectives. For the last few minutes he'd been standing by the door, chewing gum, listening to the proceedings, and eyeing the incident board with interest. "All he's got is a bag of fingers. Anyone would think it was the crime of the century."

"He does a good job. So keep your sarky comments to yourself. He's a good boss with a good team." She tapped his chest lightly. "And it's not just a bag of fingers, either. It's probably murder." This was confirmed with a nod. "Jealous, Thorpe?" She smirked. "That fat lazy sod you work for wouldn't know where to start." She was referring to Detective Inspector Brad Long.

"That 'fat lazy sod' would just round up the bloody lot of them and have done with it," Thorpe snorted. "Time in the cells, that's what the animals need." He sidled away, back to his own desk.

"He doesn't sound very impressed." Dodgy was watching him go.

"Take no notice. He's all mouth and suit, that one. They'd give a month's salary to have the clear-up rate our team's got."

Chapter 4

She was just sat there, on the pavement outside the café, smoking. Why? Why was Kelly dressed like that? She looked like a common tart in that top, that ultra-short skirt . . . and why the apron? Suddenly he understood — she must work there. She'd got herself a job serving greasy burgers and coffee in that back-street shit hole. That's why her hair was scraped back in that unflattering way. But why would she do that? Why would she need to get a job, and what had she done with the kid?

He felt the nerves start. His hands were shaking, and that sick feeling in his stomach was back again. This was all his fault. He watched her take a last pull on the cigarette. He watched as she threw it to the floor, stubbed it out and then straight away, sparked up another one. She was chain smoking. Had he driven her to this? With her hair like that she looked all pinched and pale. She was frightened.

He hated that idea. What was she afraid of? She'd nothing to fear, not from him, he would never harm her, not after what she'd done for him — for them.

Why the job? He didn't want her to work; she shouldn't have to. He tapped his fingers on the steering wheel and thought. Why, why, why? She needs the money

— of course she does; she has to eat. That must be it. Ice couldn't provide anymore, could he?

All his fault — all his fault. The words filled his head, mocking him and blocking out the noise of the traffic. He had to think. He had to think fast; he had to do something to make it right for her.

The traffic lights changed, he'd have to go, move off. One last look, and she was still sat there, still smoking. He knew what to do now. It came to him in a flash. He'd give her the money, Ice's money.

* * *

Malcolm Masheda's tall frame swaggered across the open ground between the tower blocks. He walked as if he owned the place. His hands were casually stuffed in his tracksuit pockets. A matching hoodie covered his head, casting his dark face into deeper shadow.

"Hey, man!" Two kids skimmed past on their bikes. "You watch where you's going."

They obviously hadn't recognised him, and that was bad. He was annoyed; his reputation must be slipping. He was losing his touch, going soft. Cuba's fault. He smiled. Cuba was a force for good, roaring into his life like a thunderbolt. She stood no nonsense — and Cuba Hassan wanted him out of the gang. She wanted him straight and clean, and she'd promised to help.

He raised his eyes to a deck ten floors up on one of the blocks and spotted them: police. Like most of the youths around here, he had built-in radar where the police were concerned. He didn't need this. He was keeping to the rules, and he didn't want dragging down the nick. Within seconds he'd swerved and dodged into the community centre housed on the ground floor of the tower block he lived in.

* * *

"This is a waste of time," Rocco said, rapping on the door again.

"Lucky break though, Julian finding that receipt."

"That remains to be seen, Dodgy," Rocco tempered. "I think we need to get moving. We need to find young Malcolm. We'll achieve nothing hanging around here waiting to hassle his mother."

"It'd be her receipt though, she'll be the one who buys the groceries. So how do you reckon the killer got hold of that particular carrier bag?"

"Stole it, acquired it," Rocco shrugged. "How many plastic bags do you see blowing in the streets around here? But a chat with Malcolm will help to clear this up."

Dodgy stuck his face to the letter box and shouted again. "There's no one there, all doors leading off the hallway are closed and there's a lot of post on the mat," he said, finally standing up.

"We've given it our best shot, maybe she's gone away." It was cold and way up here on the tenth floor the wind blew right through you. Rocco turned his collar up and shivered.

"We could wait," Dodgy suggested.

Rocco shook his head — no way, not in this weather. The lad was green, they couldn't afford the luxury of hanging around, but he'd learn. This was a big deal for the newbie. His first major case. He'd want to prove he could keep up — want to impress.

But the truth of the matter was that Rocco wasn't particularly concerned about missing Mrs Masheda. It was her son they needed to see. If anyone in this family was involved, then it would be Malcolm. He took out one of his cards from his overcoat pocket, scribbled a few words on the back, and pushed it through the letter box.

Ten floors up and no working lift. How in the world did the tenants manage? He looked up at the further dozen or more floors above them. This place was hell, and not just because of the gangs.

The sound of women arguing filled the air as they reached the ground floor, and both men looked around. The community centre was the venue for the Housing Action Group today, and the place was bouncing with activity. Anyone from the estate with a beef was sounding off about everything that was wrong with the place.

Rocco looked in through the tinted window. The poor sods. This place; no chance of escape, and now a maniac on the loose. He couldn't help wondering which one of those irate women had spawned the monster.

"Make for the car." He nodded to Dodgy as they strolled towards the Vauxhall.

Rocco had spotted him. The young man they were after had darted under a table as he looked in. What did young Mr Masheda have to hide?

Close to where his car was parked stood a clutter of tall rubbish bins. He pulled Dodgy in beside him and waited. Minutes later, Malcolm Masheda walked past, clutching a young woman's hand.

Despite any reservations Rocco had about Masheda he had to admit that they made a handsome couple. Both of them were tall and of West Indian descent.

"A word, please, Malcolm." Rocco flashed his warrant card. "Why are you trying to avoid us?"

"I'm not!" The young man tucked his arm around the girl's waist.

"You spotted us and disappeared into the community centre, Mash. Why would you do that if you weren't trying to avoid us?"

"I went inside to get Cuba," referring to the girl.

"Yeah, he's right," she confirmed. "And he ain't done nowt, so leave him be."

"Have you seen your friend Ice recently?" Dodgy broke in.

"He's not been around, he's hiding, inne." Mash and the girl laughed.

"Why does he have to hide? What's he done?"

"He's frightened, that's what. He doesn't want Kelly to find him and make him go back to her," Cuba sneered. "They've got a kid and Ice ain't interested, not in her and not in the kid."

"When exactly was the last time you saw him?"

"Dunno — can't remember." Mash shrugged.

"He was at that party a week ago. The one in Roxy's flat," Cuba confirmed.

"Are you sure it was a week ago?"

The girl nodded.

"When were you last on the Circle Road, Mash — down on the common?"

"Don't go there, boss." Mash shook his head.

"You seem very sure."

The young man loosened his grip on Cuba for a moment, and lifted the right leg of his tracksuit bottoms.

"I's tagged," he grimaced. "So I's not allowed to go certain places and the common is one of them and I's not allowed out before eight in the morning or after seven thirty at night."

"For how long?"

"The last five weeks. You check, you'll see I'm not lying."

Rocco had every intention of doing just that. If Masheda had nothing to do with this, then why the business with the receipt? Who wanted him stuck in their sights like this?

"Not him, then?" Dodgy said when they were back in the car, heading towards the nick.

"He has friends." Rocco was grim. "That young woman for a start: Cuba Hassan. The two of them know everything that goes on back there." He sighed. "But they won't talk to us, not properly. But I think you're right. Not him." He shrugged. "But that doesn't mean he doesn't know something useful, or hasn't heard something on the street. They stick together like glue when it suits them."

* * *

Calladine and Ruth went to Fieldfare House first, and knocked on Kelly Griggs's front door.

"She's out!" a female voice hollered at them from the open door of the next flat. "Surprised she's got the energy. That kid of hers screams most of the night. Stupid bitch should never have had him."

With that she went back inside and slammed the door shut.

"Charming." Ruth was peering through a small window beside the door. "If she's not here then there's not much we can do, I guess."

Calladine's mobile sounded.

"Looks like Rocco and Dodgy had no luck either. I'll arrange for a uniformed officer to keep an eye open until someone shows up. We'd better see if Donna Edwards is home." He shook his head wearily.

He'd tell her that her son had met with an accident, and they were looking for him. But what was the betting they'd back soon enough to tell her he was dead?

They took the stairs down. Kelly lived on the third floor, so it wasn't too arduous. They walked across the large soulless square and into another block, where Donna lived. No lifts yet again, and this time they had seven flights to climb. They had no luck there either. All three were out — or missing. He felt the familiar knot in his stomach.

The two detectives walked back across the square to their parked car. A group of youths stood against the railings, staring, following their every step. The entire pack were clones of each other: hooded tops, expensive trainers, even down to the sullen expressions plastered across their young faces.

"You know what this is, don't you? It's learn your lesson time from old man Fallon. You should speak to Central, see what he's been up to. I'll lay odds Ice was getting too big for his boots and Fallon took him down.

You'll see; whatever was going on will stop now. There won't be any more trouble, not after this."

"It's all too elaborate for Fallon." Calladine shook his head.

"Community centre," Ruth noted, as they ran the gauntlet of cat-calls and abuse on the way back to their car. "Something on, by the sound of things."

"Housing Action, but it's breaking up now." And he made towards the doors.

It was possible that he'd find one of the women in here. If not at the housing meeting, then perhaps making use of the other facilities the centre offered. There was a crèche, a café, even a food bank, and a large IT suite, which had rows of PCs, as well as superfast broadband. A couple of years back the centre had received a lottery grant and, against all the odds, had managed to hang on to the equipment that had been bought.

The two detectives walked through the centre, finishing at the IT suite. There were a few teenagers playing games, a man looking through the job sites, and Malcolm Masheda and his girlfriend giggling over a computer in the far corner.

"Afternoon, boss," he greeted them in his deep voice. "I'm a popular guy today." He grinned. "Had a couple of your mates over earlier. But I put them right. No worries, I'm job hunting, that's what we're doing, innit, girl?" He clutched Cuba somewhere around her hips. "Now I's got a CV. Cuba's been helping me." He said this proudly, sending the document to the printer.

Malcolm Masheda with a job. That was the most improbable thing Calladine had heard in a while. He stood for a moment and looked around. The kids were laughing now. They were quite content to be indoors, away from trouble and engrossed in some mindless act of violence, at one remove on a computer screen. Mash and the other guy were both job hunting. What was going on? Where was the tension? This was supposed to be an estate in turmoil.

Barbaric acts of brutality had been perpetrated on two of their number. So if they were all living in fear of Ray Fallon's wrath, why the smiling faces? Why so laid back?

In silence, Calladine walked back outside, stood at the edge of the square and looked around. Apart from the moody group of youths, who were now kicking an empty drink can around, he was surrounded by the normal sounds of day to day life. Kids, adult chatter, folk sweeping the decks, even the paper boy was delivering — and whistling as he worked. This wasn't a place in the grip of fear, far from it.

It was clear to him that they didn't know. The folk on this estate had no idea what had happened. Something wasn't right. If Ice had crossed a line and had been punished for it, then they'd all know. He felt his stomach flip again.

"Ruth!" he called to his sergeant as she joined him outside. "Would you mind hanging around for a bit, see if either of those women return home? I'll send Dodgy to join you."

Calladine had things to think about, and he needed to be alone for a bit. It wasn't a turf war, not a fight for supremacy on the drug-dealing front — so what was going on? Calladine had an idea, but it didn't sit well. His instinct was at it again.

Someone was getting rid of the rubbish.

* * *

Back at the station, Calladine went to the main office and added Masheda, Donna and Kelly's names to the incident board. He needed to talk to the two women. For his own peace of mind, he needed to ensure they were okay.

Something was wrong, he could smell it. This was all too easy. Masheda, the receipt left conveniently for them to find; it smacked of someone leading them in entirely the wrong direction.

He went to his office, retrieved the photo of Richard Pope from his file and stuck it on the incident board with the others. He didn't know why. There was no rational explanation for it being there, but he felt sure the shooting was connected in some way. That was where it had all begun.

"We've had a call, sir." Imogen burst into the office, with Julian in tow.

She was pale. Julian had his arm around her shoulder, in a gesture of comfort.

"From the charity shop in Leesdon, you know, the one in the High Street," she continued, almost faltering. "They've received a package. A bundle wrapped in a carrier bag was stuffed into a black bin liner along with a load of old clothes."

"What makes it our business?" Calladine tore his eyes reluctantly from the board.

"The carrier bag's from the same supermarket. There's a receipt clipped to it with that mark stamped on it." She nodded at the image of a bloodied hand. "And the bundle . . ." She coughed nervously. "It's a human head."

Chapter 5

Myrtle Stanley had worked at the charity shop for more than five years. It wasn't really work because it was unpaid. She was a volunteer. A volunteer who put in the hours, did the early shift, the cleaning, the sorting, anything and everything in fact to ensure that the shop stayed open and attracted people through the door.

That was their first priority, Doreen, the manageress, was fond of telling them. Like some sort of female Svengali she exerted a strange power over her well-intentioned workforce. So much so, that they all gave their time freely for the cause. Her word was law, and they happily worked like Trojans on the upkeep of the shop.

Myrtle had opened up today. She'd got out of the taxi, paid the driver, fished in her ample handbag for the shop keys, and let herself in. There was the usual array of black bags full of stuff, stacked on the steps outside the door. She'd viewed them with a mix of pleasure and dread. People were so generous; a trait Doreen had instilled in the local population. But that number of bags meant a mountain of work, and Myrtle knew today was going to be hard.

One by one she'd dragged the bags inside. It was raining, and they were already covered in drizzle, so she had to be quick. She wanted to get the clothes out and sorted before they got too damp.

It wasn't long before Wilfred joined her; another keen helper who used the shop as escape from a life of loneliness in his flat.

"You get the kettle on," she'd told him. "A strong cuppa, then we'll do these."

"Something smells a bit ripe," Wilfred had warned as he hobbled through to the small kitchen. His knee was giving him trouble again.

"I can't smell anything." Myrtle got on with organising the bags in order of size. "We mustn't quibble; we should be glad of anything we get, given the state of things around here."

She was right; they should be very grateful. More and more of the adult population were out of work. Shops in town were closing down, and a local factory had shut only last month.

That made their position in the community so much more important. They were needed. People relied on them, particularly the mothers with children to clothe. Recently they'd started a school uniform section, and that was very popular.

"Do you want me to deal with whatever it is?" Wilfred had offered, coming back into the shop with two steaming mugs. "You can't smell anything because of your trouble," he'd reminded her pointedly. "It could be something obnoxious, a dead rat or worse."

"Don't be silly, no one would do anything like that."

"Don't forget last month, and those hooligans who all but ransacked the place."

"Didn't get much though, did they? Not once we started on them."

"I got my knee knocked though, didn't I? That thug hit me with a flaming bat, could have broken it."

"A couple T-shirts, that's all they got away with in the end. It could have been much worse but we showed them." At this, she raised her fist and punched in the air.

It was then that Wilfred had taken the scissors to the offending bag, and snipped it open. He'd reeled back, covering his face with a hand as the smell hit him.

"God in Heaven, whatever is it? Myrtle, even you should be able to smell that!"

Myrtle had tried. She'd sniffed the air but had only caught a faint whiff of the unpleasantness. "There are times when Parkinson's is a blessing," she'd joked.

She'd taken Wilfred's walking stick and poked the bag hard until it gaped open. At that point the bag had fallen on its side and something had rolled out onto the carpet with a dull thud. She'd been about to send Wilfred for a dustpan and brush when she realised that the offending object was a human head.

At which point Myrtle fainted and Wilfred had called the police.

* * *

"She's been taken to the hospital, sir," Dodgy told Calladine, when he arrived at the shop. "She was shaken up and felt woozy. Had to be on the safe side, being the age she is."

"This is Doreen Potter, the manageress," Wilfred said. "I could smell something was wrong straight away, but Myrtle has Parkinson's you see. It's taken away her sense of smell, so she didn't realise."

"I was here before Doc Hoyle, sir." Ruth emerged from the kitchen with two cups of tea. "There was a lot of decomposition, but it was Ice." She gave the cups to Wilfred and Doreen. "Batho's lot have taken the receipt and the bag. I came here the moment I got the call. Donna Edwards didn't come home, nor Kelly, so it was no use hanging about on the estate."

"We need to speak to those women as a matter of urgency. I need to know Edwards's movements over these last few days, and when he was last seen alive. We could do with knowing if he's upset anyone recently, too."

"A quick visit to the Hobfield, and I'll write you a long list," Ruth was sarcastic. "It's more a case of who hasn't he upset."

"What about Masheda?"

"Convenient that, wasn't it?" Calladine put on a pair of gloves. "A receipt we can trace straight back to that family without any waste of time." He shook his head. "Someone's playing us, Ruth, and I don't like it."

Calladine sighed — he could tell from Ruth's expression that she didn't entirely go along with this train of thought. She was familiar with this mood; she'd seen it before often enough. Calladine knew she considered him a damn good cop, but his big failing was this tendency to let his mind go off at a tangent, and keep things to himself. So what to tell her?

If this wasn't gang or Fallon related, then what was it? Ruth seemed to think that this was a drugs war, pure and simple. It was a case of Ice having overstepped the mark in a fight for supremacy. It had got out of hand and Ice was dead. But was that true? Calladine needed to talk to Fallon.

"This leaving body parts where they are sure to be found is showmanship — a warning to others. To us," Ruth told him.

"Perhaps," was Calladine's cryptic reply.

"You look puzzled, sir." She approached him. "Perhaps we should do what Thorpe suggested and go round up the entire bunch of them."

"This isn't a turf war, Ruth. We're supposed to think it is —" He looked at her. "But they've overdone it; they've gone too far." He was convinced of it, but he could tell he wasn't reaching her. He closed his eyes for a moment. Turf war. It would almost be a relief, given how things were going. But his instincts told him that this was something far worse.

Calladine shook his head and looked around the shop. It was well laid out and offered a wide range of stuff. Not bad, considering everything was second-hand. He wandered past the lines of clothing and sat down on the bench next to Wilfred.

"You were very brave," he told the elderly man gently. "You did everything right, ringing us, not touching things. I know you're in the village and not on the estate, but do the kids give you any trouble?"

"Not usually, but last week we had a group of them in. Tried to rubbish the place." He wiped his brow with a cotton hankie. "Me and Myrtle saw them off, hooligans that they were."

Calladine couldn't imagine what had gone through the man's mind when the head had rolled onto the floor. It was shocking, horrific — almost inconceivable that anyone would leave it in a place where they must have known how it would be found.

But wasn't that the point? Whoever had done this wanted it found, same with the fingers. They'd been left where their quick discovery was assured.

Calladine's eyes narrowed. This was brutal. "Where's Rocco?" he asked Ruth.

"He's gone to check the other shops down the High Street on the hunt for CCTV again. The bag must have been left between six last night and nine this morning."

"Has the . . . body part gone to the doc?" Calladine tried hard not to visualise this particular part.

Ruth nodded. "The doc was here within fifteen minutes. He took it away pretty smartish." She swallowed audibly.

He turned to Wilfred. "Do you have CCTV here? Perhaps outside?"

Doreen answered. "No cameras, I'm afraid. We're a charity shop, Inspector, so we shouldn't need them."

Calladine would have liked to lecture her on personal safety, as well as the benefits for folk like him when things went wrong, but he didn't bother.

"We don't have an assault any more, we have a full blown murder on our hands," he told Ruth quietly. "When he feels up to it, I want Wilfred interviewed formally, and someone will have to go and see Mrs Stanley."

"I can go." Ruth volunteered. "I'll get their statements tomorrow, and bring them back to the station."

Chapter 6

Calladine had said five, but it was way past seven by the time the team reassembled in the main office, which had now become the incident room. He yawned, checking his watch.

"Make sure a PC is keeping an eye on that flat. I want to know the minute Donna gets home. I don't care what time it is. I'll speak to her myself. Any joy with the CCTV?"

Imogen Goode shook her head and sighed. She'd spent most of the day with her eyes glued to the damned screen, but she didn't know what she was looking for. What constituted suspicious behaviour around here? Watching the goings on at the shops on the Hobfield opened a window into another world. She'd seen at least two scuffles and one failed mugging. And all within the space of two hours' worth of tape.

"I'll keep at it."

"We're definitely looking at murder," Calladine announced to his team. "Ice might have managed without his fingers, but he'll not get by without his head. I'm doubtful this is gang related, but keep an open mind. Ian Callum Edwards is a victim for sure, but I've also got grave doubts regarding the fate of Gavin Hurst. The two lived in each other's pockets. However, there's always the chance that Gavin knows something and is holed up somewhere. We need people to talk. I want a presence on the Hobfield, the community centre in particular."

Whispers went around the room. He knew what they'd be thinking. Not gang related? What was he getting at? If this wasn't gang warfare, then what was it? He saw Ruth shake her head and fold her arms. In her opinion he was doing it again — ignoring the obvious.

Calladine wrote Gavin's name on the board. "Why hasn't Julian come up with his name?"

"No DNA on record," Imogen offered.

Calladine gave her a look and narrowed his eyes. That was information for him and the team, not gossip for Julian and Imogen to chew over.

"Speak to his family, friends, anyone who saw — sees him regularly. We need to know a lot more about Gavin."

"Gavin doesn't seem to have any family," Ruth told the team. "He was living with an auntie until she died. After that he's had no fixed address. If you ask me he's been dossing down with Ice somewhere."

"Rocco, try and find out where, and anything you can about any other relatives he might have. Speak to them. If they're local they might have had contact with him recently. Kelly Griggs — any ideas?"

"The kid is in nursery most days, so I presume she's found herself a job. Her neighbours don't know where. No one's seen her for a day or two," Rocco added.

"We need to speak to both women," he reiterated. "Four of us have been on the Hobfield today, and I didn't sense any tension. In fact the place was surprisingly quiet. Even Masheda and his girlfriend didn't seem bothered to be seen talking to us. Now that's not natural."

He paused for a moment. The nick might have got a rude awakening from the quiet summer, but the estate hadn't caught up yet. The problems would only get worse when it did. All hell would break out between the gangs.

They'd blame each other for Ice's death. There'd be beatings, fighting, and the police would have to pick up the pieces.

"Once this gets out we'll struggle to keep a lid on the violence, so we need to move fast. Today's been a long, hard slog. We've no motive, no weapons, and no idea why these two were killed. Was it deliberate or random? But we do have names, well one for sure. Tomorrow I want some background. I want everything we can get on Ice and Gavin Hurst." He looked back at the board. "While we're at it, see if there is any link, no matter how tenuous, to Richard Pope."

Minutes later, the team dispersed for the day.

"Are you going?" Ruth asked Calladine, looking up from her desk. "I'll finish up myself in a while, but I've still got some stuff to do. I want to make some inroads into my research on Ice's background. He had a record. He'd spent time in a Young Offenders Unit. You never know — there might be something in there that will help," Ruth nodded hopefully. "Something to make you see the reality of the situation. Make you see that this was to do with drugs and gang rivalry, and not the work of some wild murderer on the loose."

"Don't stay too late. Your day's been as long as mine. Mind you I'm off to see my mother first, then home." He yawned. "I'll see you tomorrow, Ruth. Then with any luck we'll interview those women."

He still hadn't done anything about Monika's present. The Antiques Centre would be closed now, so it'd have to wait. Her birthday wasn't until the end of the week anyway. He needed to think, but his head was full of clutter. Monika was only part of it; there was also his mother. She was old and frail. He saw as much of her as he could, but he still felt guilty about the situation. He knew this couldn't continue. One day soon he'd get the call, and he'd feel even worse for not having done more. But at least he'd got her into the home, a good one. The residents were well looked after, Monika saw to that. He had no worries on that score.

* * *

Well looked after and kept warm. In fact the place was so hot the air hit him like a blow torch as he went through the front doors. It was a sauna. No fear of his mother freezing to death, not in here. Calladine walked down the corridor towards the sitting room, shuffling his overcoat from his shoulders as he went.

"Tom!" Monika greeted him, coming out of her office.

She was a few inches shorter than he, and struggling with her weight. Her dark hair was beginning to grey down the parting. She looked tired; like him she had a lot on her plate.

"You look beat." She frowned, cupping his weary face in her hands. "Trouble?"

"Could be." He nodded. "In fact, yes, big trouble, my instincts are telling me. I'll look in on Ma, then finally I can get back home."

Monika kissed him on the mouth and stroked his cheek. He put his arm around her waist and held her close for a moment. This brief moment of affection made Calladine uncomfortable.

What was wrong with him?

Monika was a good woman; he could do a lot worse. He should think more about settling down properly, and he'd known her for a good while. But was that enough? There was a time when their relationship had been vibrant; when she sparked something in him. But since their last breakup things had changed — she'd changed. She'd aged, and put on the weight. She carried it well because she was tall, but it was there nonetheless. He was a selfish prick. This woman was the closest thing he'd had to a girlfriend in years, and he had the temerity to be picky.

"She's not been well today. Her legs are bad again," Monika warned. "They've been bandaged, and she's grumpy and a bit confused. I asked the doctor to see her, and he left some medication."

"Her legs?"

"Cellulitis, Tom. It's common enough in the elderly when they're sitting around a lot."

"Confusion . . ." He shook his head. "She used to be as sharp as a pin." This was something he found hard to adjust to. He was aware that she was forgetting things more and more; he just didn't want to admit that she was slipping further away from him.

"We'll keep an eye on her, don't worry." Monika was reassuring. "She's in there." She nodded towards the sitting room. "Watching the telly and drinking tea."

"Look, I might be busy this week." He was paving the way for his probable absence. "I'll arrange something for your birthday though. I won't forget, I promise. A meal at that Italian, the one that does the wonderful Carbonara?" he suggested hopefully.

"Suits me. Perhaps you'd consider staying over at mine too. Give a girl a proper treat." She winked at him.

Calladine bent down and brushed her lips with his own. He smiled and nodded, but he'd have to think about that one. He knew already he'd make some excuse and duck out of it. He didn't know what it was, but since they'd rekindled this relationship, he'd kept Monika very much at arm's length.

It wasn't that he didn't like her, because he did. At one time he'd positively lusted after her. But that was a long time ago, when she'd been married to Ruth's brother. Perhaps it had been a case of simply wanting what he couldn't have. These days she was more of a friend, a comfort, even a sounding board. That was no basis for a relationship. He knew his faults, and relationships with women were high on the list. He'd been married and divorced, both before his twenty-first birthday. He'd made

55

mistakes, always put the job first, and he doubted he could change now.

They were sat in a semi-circle, in huge high-backed chairs with footrests. His mother sat at the end, so he was able to crouch down beside her.

"You're not so good . . ." He reached for her hand. She didn't respond, didn't even acknowledge his presence. As Monika had said, her legs were bandaged, but she seemed comfortable enough.

It had happened quickly. One day she'd been running her own life and doing her best to organise his, then, as if a switch had been flicked, she was here. As care homes went, this place was fine, more than fine, with the added bonus of having Monika in charge. But it wasn't how he'd imagined his mother would end up.

He patted her thin, bony hand. Her skin was like paper, wrinkled and covered in brown stains. Age: he still couldn't get his head around it. When had this happened, when had things changed so much?

* * *

Kelly Griggs stirred, groaning into the darkness. She flicked the switch on the lamp by her bed, and cursed as the bulb blew. She rolled over, groaned again and clamped her hands to her ears in self-defence. The tiny bedroom was filled with a crescendo of noise, that high-pitched wail that only a baby was capable of making. It was the sort of wail that demanded instant attention.

The young girl rolled across the bed and rubbed her tired eyes. In the Moses basket beside her on the floor she could just make out the hungry bundle wriggling with impatience as he thrust tiny fists into a sucking mouth. Hungry as he was, Jack would have to wait until she sorted his milk. Kelly felt around on the cabinet beside her bed for cigarettes and her lighter.

She'd have to see to him, she decided, lighting a cigarette and moving carefully in the dark bedroom towards the kitchen. Very soon the inhabitants of the entire deck would be awake and on her back, and she couldn't risk that. Her neighbours were difficult enough to get on with as it was.

It was the middle of the night. There was just no way she could keep this up, the same exhausting routine, week after week. She stumbled across the floor and heard a *knock, knock* from the adjoining flat.

"The old biddy's awake now," Kelly told the screaming babe. The elderly woman next door was using her stick to rap on the wall, trying to stir her into action.

"For God's sake feed him, Kelly!" The walls must be made of cardboard, she thought, running a hand through her long, dark hair in exasperation.

"You've got the whole deck up now, you lazy cow!" There was a final thump on the wall.

She wasn't lazy, she was tired, exhausted by the drudgery of it all. She had an infant to care for, and a new job to hold down. Ice had said he'd help. He'd promised her the day Jack was born that he wouldn't let her down. That was three months ago, and she could count on the fingers of one hand the number of times she'd seen him since.

Kelly lit a gas ring in the small kitchen, flicking on the light as she went. She poured the contents of a feed she'd made earlier into a pan for it to heat, while she lifted the distraught infant from his bed.

She heard a knock, a rap at her front door. Bloody neighbours were taking this too far. Young babies cry, there wasn't anything she could do about that.

"Bugger off!" she screamed, as she rocked Jack in her arms. Moments later she had transferred the milk to a feeding bottle and stuck it in his mouth. He was quiet at last. Kelly would give whoever had come to her door a right roasting. She was in the mood.

But the deck corridor was empty and the surrounding flats were dark and quiet. Whoever knocked had legged it sharpish. Then looking down, she saw it. A grotty-looking carrier bag, tied up with pink ribbon and with a note attached, had been dumped on her doorstep.

Someone playing tricks; something loathsome left as payback for the noise? She was tempted to put it straight in the bin, but instead Kelly picked the thing up and plonked it on the table, undoing it with her one free hand.

What she saw made her blink in disbelief. It wasn't something obnoxious after all, not by a long chalk. Someone had left a bag full of money on her doorstep. A bag full of money tied up with pretty pink ribbon, she thought, feeling the smoothness of the fabric against her fingers.

She tipped it onto the table, watching it roll around in small tubular bundles fastened up with elastic bands. Ice, she thought immediately. That was how he kept his money. He'd roll it up then hide it on his body, in his pockets, and even down his socks.

Why? Why would he do this? Why not just knock and come in? Why not give her the money in person? Up until now he hadn't given her a penny, which was why she was slaving away in that café every spare minute she had.

She unravelled the note. It was scrawled in red biro. *You did a kind thing.* What did that mean? What kind thing? When was that?

He must be in some sort of trouble and he didn't want her to be involved. He was being considerate. But Ice wasn't considerate; it wasn't Ice at all. He could talk a good game, but that's all it was, talk, like when Jack was born. So what was this? Why all this money, and why not show himself?

Chapter 7

Tuesday

He was drifting somewhere between sleep and thoughts of his mother. She was calling to him, pressing that damn buzzer thing she sometimes wore around her neck. Freda Calladine wasn't happy . . . but for some reason she wasn't able to tell him why.

The sound was louder, piercing and close. Calladine shook himself suddenly, realising what it was. He fumbled for a moment with the duvet, then reached a hand over to his bedside table and picked up his throbbing mobile. The screen said *Ruth*.

"I'm on my way to the common. More body parts have turned up. It's a truly horrible mess, according to the constable who contacted me."

"Okay, I'll meet you there." He was suddenly wide awake, unsure if he'd slept or not. There was too much on his mind — his mother, Monika and, of course, the case.

He'd known it was only a matter of time before this happened. Whoever was responsible couldn't hang onto the bodies for long, it wasn't practical. Sooner or later the rest of those poor sods were bound to surface. Calladine supposed that their man hadn't been too concerned about where he'd left the other bits, so the common was as good a place as any.

* * *

Ruth turned her collar up. It was cold and raining hard. The ground was soggy with mud and churned by numerous pairs of feet. She hated all this early morning excitement. A rushed breakfast eaten on the hoof and a cup of tea downed in one. She couldn't wait to get back to the office, to some warmth and a chance to eat properly.

She and Rocco carefully picked their way towards one of the small police tents that had been erected on the wasteland that was Leesdon Common. They made lonely, forlorn shapes in the open wilderness. A sad place to end up, she thought, shivering.

It was early, not yet six in the morning, but still a crowd had gathered, their necks craning behind the police tape, all curious to know what had happened. How had they got to hear about it? She'd like to know how Calladine was going to keep this quiet.

The edge of the Hobfield estate was only a few hundred yards away from Leesdon centre. A tract of wasteland, known as the common, separated them. It sloped down from the outskirts of Leesdon to a small stream at its lowest point then turned upwards again towards the estate. The locals used it as a shortcut to the shops along Leesdon High Street. The kids used it as a place to dump and torch stolen cars.

"Time to get kitted up." She took the proffered paper forensic suit and climbed into it. She pulled on the over-socks and snapped on a pair of latex gloves. Once ready, she pulled back the door flap of the nearest tent. DI Calladine would be here shortly. In the meantime, it was her call. She was flattered that he trusted her to be thorough. It had taken her long enough to earn that trust.

Ruth Bayliss entered the tent totally unprepared for the sight that confronted her. The remains of what she was later to learn were two dismembered bodies lay scattered over the wet ground.

She clasped her hand over her mouth to stifle a scream. Unprofessional, but she couldn't help herself. Gavin Hurst's head was lying like a football at her feet. One of his eyes was gone, and most of his teeth. He'd obviously been severely battered about the face.

It was a scene from a bad horror film. There was just so much blood, too many entrails, so much muddy, red pulp everywhere. In that moment, Ruth knew that Calladine's instincts had been correct. This wasn't the work of Fallon or a rival gang. This was something else entirely. She closed her eyes for a moment, trying to steady herself, and understood exactly what the inspector had feared. This was the work of a maniac.

Ruth had seen many horrific crimes, but nothing matched this. She inched forward carefully; what looked like guts were spread over the ground in front of her.

"Nasty, isn't it?" Doc Hoyle understated. "We've erected four tents and there are body parts in each. Spread over quite an area too. It looks like someone has come along with plastic bags full of bloody waste, and strewn it all over the common."

Ruth swallowed hard. She couldn't tell how Rocco was doing, but she'd seen enough to make her feel faint. She stepped forward, tentatively, trying to avoid both the empty bags and the blood, until she felt the ground squish and give under her foot. She looked at Rocco. His eyes held hers for a moment. After a breath or two she steeled herself to glance down, and was horrified to find she'd just stood on a human kidney.

* * *

Calladine slammed the car door shut and plunged his hands deep into his raincoat pockets, hiding his fists. His face was drawn, hard-looking and expressionless as he walked towards one of the tents. Ruth was coming out in a hurry.

By the time he got to her she was behind the tent, almost bent double.

"First time since I was a rookie," she apologised. "Couldn't help it. It's dreadful in there . . ." She nodded towards the tent. "And there's more — entrails in that one and severed limbs over there."

"No half measures then."

Calladine lifted the tent flap and looked inside. Doctor Hoyle was bent over a torso. He looked up.

"I'll get them back to the mortuary, Tom. While they're out here I can't even tell which part belongs to which body. Although I take it the hand over there with all the fingers missing belongs to your Mr Edwards."

"Why here?" Calladine closed his eyes against the sight. "No attempt's been made to hide anything."

"That's about the size of it. Dumped here — left in all their gory glory for some poor unsuspecting bastard to find. The body parts were brought here in carrier bags and emptied out all over the place. God knows what it's all about. I don't envy you your job, Tom . . . Oh, and you should know. That bloodied hand mark was stamped on some of the bags and body parts."

Calladine wasn't surprised at Ruth's reaction. He was perilously close to throwing up himself. He finished his round of the tents and stood in the damp morning air, inhaling deeply. This was as bad as it got. But what had he got? Two mutilated, murdered bodies and a mark. Was it a gang tag? No it wasn't — it definitely wasn't that. But the bastard doing this wanted him to think it was. He wanted them all to be chasing shadows.

"Detective Inspector?" The voice interrupting his thoughts was soft.

Calladine opened his eyes and stared at the young woman in front of him. She was young — well, a good few years younger than he, and blonde. He'd never seen her before and her accent wasn't local.

"Lydia Holden from the Leesworth Echo." She took a card from her bag. "Can you give me anything? The heads up on what's going on here?"

If she hadn't been a woman he'd have told her to piss off. He wasn't in the mood. But she was, and his mother had brought him up to be a gentleman, so he pursed his lips and shook his head.

"You shouldn't be here. Behind the tape is where you belong."

"I'll get nothing back there."

"As yet there's nothing to tell, and you should know better, Miss . . ."

"Holden." She continued to smile. "This is so very extraordinary." Her gesture encompassed the crowded scene. "I can count, Inspector," she dipped her eyelashes, ". . . and there are four tents. I've seen the pathologist arrive. So am I to take it you're dealing with more than one murder here?"

He gave her a long hard look.

"You can take it any way you want. I've said nothing about murder, and I can't discuss details yet, so you're wasting your time." Calladine shook his head. He'd like to tell this woman to go to hell, but he knew his public relations. Nonetheless, he had to tell her something; the press would be all over this soon in any case. In no time they'd be clinging to him like leeches. "We're dealing with an incident, Miss Holden, for now that's all I can say. When I have more I'll be in touch."

He nodded curtly. As he tried to sidestep her, she caught hold of his arm.

"I'm not stupid, Inspector. This is something big. You can't kid me."

The sweet smile had soon vanished. She was just another hack after scandal. She'd be wasting her time using those looks to get anything out of him.

"It could be in your interest to give the story to me first. We could help each other. You can't keep us out of this, Inspector. I suspect it's too big."

Lydia Holden wasn't a name he recognised. The local reporter he usually dealt with was a crusty old character called Morton. What had happened to him? He frowned and looked at her. He wasn't happy; it was early and he hadn't slept. This woman, whoever she was, was a nuisance he could do without. But she was right. He would be able to keep the press at arm's length for just so long.

She smiled again. Her teeth were white and she had sparkling blue eyes. Her blonde hair billowed in soft curls around delicate features. The more she smiled at him, the more he couldn't tear his eyes away.

Lydia Holden met his stare. She was probably aware of the effect she was having on him; most men would find her beguiling. Tom Calladine was no different. She coughed lightly and finally succeeded in handing over her card. "We'll talk again, Inspector. My instincts tell me that before this is finished you're going to need all the help you can get."

Chapter 8

"Mrs Edwards? Donna?"

"What the hell do you want, this time in the morning?" She'd seen at once that he was police. Her hands rested on scrawny hips, and a cigarette hung from her crudely painted mouth.

"May we come in, Donna?" This isn't something we should discuss out here." He was aware of faces peering at them from the neighbour's front doors.

She shook her head in disgust and discarded the fag, letting it fall over the railing. Calladine watched it flicker and spin to the ground seven floors below.

"I can tell you now I've got nowt to say. Nowt about me and nowt about that son of mine. And it's Miss, not Mrs."

Calladine, Ruth and a uniformed female officer followed her inside the untidy, poky flat.

"I'm afraid I've got bad news for you, Donna."

This was never easy. It was the worst part of his job and it never got any better. Even if it was a son like Ice, it wasn't a task he relished. She might look like a hard nut, but it was always a front. This was a rough place to live, and the Hobfield Estate gave no quarter. If you didn't have a big mouth, if you didn't fight back, then you had no chance.

Donna Edwards looked like a volatile woman. She probably knew this visit meant trouble, and she was on edge. She busied herself, nervously knocking a couple of cushions into shape and throwing them back onto the sofa.

"What's the little bastard done now?" She grabbed another cigarette from a pack on the table. "If it's anything to do with money then it's no good looking at me, cos I've got none. No good little scroat should be working. He owes me, and then there's Kelly and that babe of hers. She was here earlier in the week, looking for him and asking for help, poor cow."

"It's nothing to do with money, Donna." He heard Ruth clear her throat behind him, wanting him to get on with it. "I'm afraid it's bad news. Ice — Ian. He is dead. He's been killed."

Donna Edwards stared at him, not quite grasping what she'd been told. The female PC walked forward and ushered her onto the sofa. Calladine watched all this happen in slow motion. Now it would begin. Within hours, perhaps less, the whole estate would know.

"Accident?" Her voice was a whisper.

At that moment Calladine wished with all his heart that it had been. The explanation would have been easy then, uncomplicated. A few words of comfort and they could leave her to get on with it. As it was, he couldn't tell her the truth, not in its unadulterated form, not yet.

"No, Donna, not an accident. I'm afraid Ian was murdered."

Her eyes went wild. She looked frantically from one officer to another, and then pushed the PC's arm from her shoulder.

"No!" she screamed. "Not Ice. He'd never let that happen. He is . . . He knew about the dangers."

"What dangers? What are you talking about, Donna?"

She stared at him with a look of pure hate and clutched the sides of her head, shrieking. "I've already said, I'm telling you nowt! He was my boy and it's not his fault."

Donna Edwards collapsed to the floor, wailing and screaming. The PC tried her best to get her to a chair, to comfort her, but it was no use.

"Donna, when did you last see Ian? I'm sorry I have to ask these questions, but the information might help us find who did this. You do want us to find out what happened to Ice, don't you?"

She stared at him with glazed eyes. She looked frightened, an added layer of distress that aroused the detective's curiosity. What was on her mind? What did she know that she wasn't saying? Ray Fallon?

"Was there anything going on? Was there a feud? Had Ice crossed someone he shouldn't, Fallon for example?"

There, he'd asked the question. Uttered the name. Calladine doubted very much she'd tell him, but he had to ask.

She shot him an angry look then shook her head. "No. He's not stupid. He'd never mess with that bastard. He knew which lines never to cross." Her voice had dropped to a whisper. "He knew well enough what Fallon's like, what'd happen if he crossed him. He runs this shithole — Fallon, not the police."

Calladine shook his head. Fallon was in Strangeways prison, so how come he was still running things on the Hobfield? Via his goons, that was how.

"Anyway, he never said nothing to nobody. Fallon trusted him. He did a good job and never put a foot wrong." She hesitated. "I would have known if he'd messed up. There are folk out there who'd be only too pleased to tell me. You've no idea what it's like round here. It's damned hard, and people are quick to hate. Plenty hated Ice because of what he did, the drugs and that . . ." She was sobbing. "But there's more that'll miss him now he's gone. No one would dare cross him, not with Fallon to call on. The place has ticked over nicely, dead quiet like, since last spring."

It has, hasn't it? thought Calladine. So what the hell was this all about?

"PC Brooke is going to stay with you. She'll arrange for someone to come and sit with you, a family member, or a friend. Don't leave the flat for the time being, Donna. If you need anything PC Brooke will arrange it."

Calladine knew Donna Edwards wouldn't like this, but he had no choice. He didn't want the press getting hold of her. He could visualise the headlines, and they made him cringe.

* * *

Calladine sat down opposite the station's other DI. He was an untidy bugger. Plastic sandwich containers, empty beer cans, and a mountain of paperwork, most of it official, littered his desk.

"Ray Fallon," he began. "You've had dealings with him recently, what's he up to?"

"He's all but finished. Washed up, that's what he's like, Tom. We reckon we've got him on that drug bust. Stupid bastard was caught with a car boot full of crack, not his usual style at all. With a bit of luck he'll go down too. But the CPS are dragging their heels, something about a witness and the evidence. Can't see it myself, banged to rights Fallon is," he shrugged. "But you know what Fallon's like, he'll bribe someone here, threaten someone there and then he'll walk. The evidence and the witness will miraculously evaporate into thin air."

There was no denying it — Fallon led a charmed life, a charmed life propped up by savagery and cash.

"He was in Strangeways. While the legal bods made up their expensive minds, he couldn't get bail. But last week the slimy toerag had a coronary so he's had to be moved to Wythenshawe Hospital. He's had a triple bypass, and won't be out for a while." He smiled and again shrugged his bulky frame. "Couldn't be better as far as we're concerned — he might even die; scum off the streets, nice one!"

Was that what had been bothering his mother? Calladine wondered. And if she didn't know, should he tell her? Fallon being so ill could give him a problem — one that had nothing at all to do with the case.

Chief Inspector George Jones walked into the office. He was carrying a couple of files under his arm and had a frown on his face. He'd been promoted to DCI within the last six months and it was obvious to everyone in the station that he found his new role heavy-going. He was thinner — probably stress, Calladine thought, and he was losing his hair.

"I need a word with you two," he began. "Murder on the Hobfield, bad business." He shook his head. "I know it's your case, Tom, but you could well end up needing some help. So in the absence of anything more important, I want you to make your people available, Brad. Okay?"

Brad Long shrugged again. He usually did what he could to help the cause, but Tom Calladine didn't always ask for his support. It wasn't his way. Calladine's working practice was a bit on the *Lone Ranger* side of things. There were times when his own team didn't even know what he was up to.

Calladine swore under his breath. The last person he wanted foisting on him was Brad-bloody-Long. The man was the butt of far too many jokes for his liking — it was his total disregard for office etiquette and all the excess weight. And he did nothing to help himself, so his lifestyle, the pies and the pints, were finally beginning to take their toll. He'd be no good to anyone in a couple of years.

"Sir, if you've got a minute, could I have a private word?"

"Sure, Tom, come into my office."

Calladine nodded at Brad and followed the Chief Inspector into his office, closing the door behind him. He didn't want anyone overhearing what he was about to say.

"I plan to visit Ray Fallon in Wythenshawe Hospital."

George Jones's face clouded. "Are you sure that's a good idea? Don't want you stepping on Central's toes, Tom. I'll have to clear it. Is this visit pertinent to the case in hand?"

"It might be. Fallon's responsible for supplying most of the drugs around the Manchester area and, of course, on the Hobfield. More importantly he ran Ice and Hurst. If there's a takeover in progress then he might say something to me that he wouldn't tell another cop." Calladine knew this was pushing it a bit. If he were honest, he was probably the last person Fallon would speak to.

Jones thought about it for a moment. Calladine's connection with Fallon was something he'd only been told about since his promotion, and even then he'd wondered if the Super had been having him on.

"I want to be able to rule Fallon in or rule him out. If I can speak to him face to face, then I'll know."

Jones raised his eyebrows, annoyed. More of the mysterious Calladine instinct. Still, if it worked . . .

"As you are aware, I can see him in an unofficial capacity. As far as Fallon is concerned it wouldn't look out of place for me to visit, given the gravity of his illness. I'll tell him I'm reporting back to my mother — he'll buy that."

"Okay, but still let me clear it first. Fallon isn't someone even you see every day. And we don't want to arouse too much interest, do we? Can you imagine the speculation if someone from the press saw you with him?"

Calladine nodded. He didn't relish the prospect of a cosy little *tête-à-tête* with one of Manchester's most notorious criminals either, but he considered it necessary.

"I'll speak to Central — get clearance, then I'll let you know. If you do go, for Heaven's sake go alone. Don't make the visit look in any way official."

* * *

"I'm going home to freshen up," Calladine told Ruth on returning to the incident room. "How about you? Do you need to take an hour after this morning and all that mud?"

"I'm okay, sir. There are showers here, you know . . ." she said, grinning. "But I'll come along for the ride. I've come up with something on Ice." She flourished a printout. "Did you know that when he was a kid, at Leesworth Comprehensive, he was implicated in the death of another pupil?"

"No, I didn't. And why, I wonder, has that little snippet been kept quiet all this time?"

"Because in the end, there was no case to answer. There wasn't enough evidence to take anything to court. But we still have the records on file, and I'm having them dug out."

They made for Calladine's vehicle in the car park. It didn't surprise him about Ice. He'd been trouble ever since he took his first steps. But Calladine had known nothing about this.

"Give those records a real close looking at, Ruth. Digging around in Ice's background could well throw up something we can use. And while you're at it, try and unpick what went wrong with the original investigation. We both knew Ice and what he was capable of. If someone thought he was responsible for the death of a kid, then the chances are he probably was."

* * *

It took less than five minutes to reach his house.

"Who was the kid?" Calladine asked, as they pulled up outside the cottage.

71

"A boy called David Morpeth. He lived on the estate too. Name ring any bells?"

"No, not a surname I know. You could find out if there's any family left around here. They might give you some info."

"I'll check. I'll check that, and speak to staff at the school."

"A kid ends up dead and everything points to Ice. I want to know why — and why the case fell through. The kid's family wouldn't have been happy about that. Someone out there could have held a grudge, all this time — wanted to get even."

"I think we'd know if that was the case, sir. Probably nothing in it, not after all this time. Just background — but interesting nonetheless."

"Make some coffee, would you? And toast if you want. I missed breakfast this morning, as well as everything else." He rubbed at his unshaven chin. "Make yourself comfortable, Ruth. I won't be long."

* * *

The detective inspector was surprisingly tidy for a man living alone. A little too tidy perhaps, Ruth thought, as she scanned the neatly placed photographs and ornaments on the mantle above the open fireplace and on the shelving unit that covered one wall.

She didn't come here often and was very curious, couldn't resist a look. Some of the photos were quite recent. Calladine and his mother, Calladine and Monika, but some were old black-and-white ones. Ruth had never met his ex-wife, Rachel, and had often wondered what she was like. She couldn't picture the serious, job-obsessed detective even *having* a wife, and so when she found one that showed him with a young woman in what was obviously a wedding gown, she pounced on it.

They looked so young — what had he said? Married and divorced before twenty-one! She was pretty, too.

Rachel Calladine was slim with long, reddish hair. What had happened to her? Was it just about being too young, or had she dumped him?

"Wish I could say they were happier times." He was drying his short hair with a towel as he came into the room. "But they weren't. Me and Rachel were a disaster. No good putting it any other way." He grimaced. "We were too young and got swept up in a tide of lust and our parents' ambition to get their offspring married off."

"She looks nice. Very pretty." Ruth put the photo back in its place. Wouldn't do to pry too deep.

He might be a good cop but he was crap at relationships and that time in his life he kept very much under wraps. Too painful — did he still hanker after his wife, his first love? Ruth had never asked and even if she did, she wouldn't get a straight answer. But she didn't like discussing her love life either — not that she had one. Ruth's current thought was that it was too late for her, plus she'd become far too independent for her own good.

"I thought I asked you to put the toast on. Never mind prying into my private life, Sergeant — we need to eat."

"Sorry, I couldn't help myself. Too nosey, I'm afraid. Do you ever see her?"

"Who, Rachel? God no, not since — well, not in the last thirty years. She moved away, Bristol I think. She probably re-married." He paused thoughtfully. "I hope she did. I wanted her to be happy. She deserved a better husband than me. I was bloody useless."

There was nothing to be said to that. Ruth had watched his so-called, *try to be better*, effort with Monika, and wasn't impressed. Goodness knows what he must have been like back then.

"I thought I'd go and talk to the staff at the school later. There must be someone left who remembers what happened to David Morpeth."

"Good idea. I'm off to Wythenshawe."

"Why? What are you up to?"

"I'm going to visit Ray Fallon in hospital. Apparently he's had a heart attack and is in a bad way."

Ruth was astonished. No one visited Ray Fallon, not without a lot of red tape. And anyway, why would anyone want to?

"What on earth for? Does Jones know? Won't that get you into bother with the Manchester force?"

"Yes, Jones knows and I'll take my chances with Manchester. They can't do much anyway. I have a distinct advantage when it comes to Fallon." He poured the coffee into two mugs.

"I'd be very careful if I were you, Tom. That man's dangerous. Well, more than dangerous, he's evil. If you annoy him you'll find yourself in very deep doodoo. I met him once, you know . . ." She shuddered. "I sat in on an interview before I came here, when I worked at Manchester. The man creeped me out. He's a smooth bastard and no mistake. He's so well mannered, so cool and sure of himself. He knew we had nothing, and he played on it. I don't envy you. To be honest I think you're just wasting your time. You'll get nothing from him."

"I'll be fine. No need to worry about me."

Ruth shot him a dubious look.

"Take a look at that photo, the one on the middle shelf, halfway along."

Ruth picked up the old, grainy, black-and-white snap. It showed a woman and two young boys. "Your mum? And one of the lads is you?"

"The one on the left is me. The one on the right is Ray Fallon."

Ruth blinked and held the photo up to the light streaming through the front window. "Good heavens, you're right! How did that happen? How come one of Manchester's most dangerous criminals is so pally with my DI?"

"Fallon is my cousin." He handed her a mug of coffee and a slice of toast. "Our mothers were sisters. When his mum died he came to live with us. Just down the road in fact, at number forty-two. From the age of eight, my mum practically brought him up."

Ruth didn't know what to say. So they were rather more than cousins, then. From what he'd just told her they were more like brothers. She looked again at the photo. The boys were laughing. They each had hold of one of Freda Calladine's hands. They seemed happy, the three of them together.

"But you're both so very different — you've turned out complete opposites." She was struggling with this new knowledge. "You're a cop, a damned good one, and he's a vicious bastard who'd shoot you dead without a flicker of conscience."

"I know exactly what he's like. I have no idea why things are the way they are. Fallon left us at sixteen, and just disappeared. When he returned in his early twenties the metamorphosis was complete. He was the monster we know now. This isn't general knowledge at the nick. I don't want it to be, either. Jones and the Super are the only two who know — and now you, of course."

"So why tell me?"

"Because I might get something from him, and then you'll need to know. I can't work on this alone, Ruth. I can get in to see him, plead the family angle. Once my mother knows what's happened she'll expect me to see him anyway. Besides you're a friend," he said, "and it's time I told you."

"Has this — your relationship with Fallon — ever caused you any problems?"

Calladine laughed. "Why do you think I've never risen above DI? Jones is a good cop, but he's younger than me and hasn't been in the job as long. Plus his clear-up rate as a DI was mediocre at best. I was overlooked, deliberately so, because of Fallon. No one says anything, but I know how things work. I can't be allowed to rise through the ranks above a certain level. Fallon is a gun-carrying murderer, a well-known gangster. And he's my bloody cousin." He slammed his empty mug down on the table.

Ruth had often wondered why Calladine had never gone for promotion. Now she knew.

"Just be careful, Tom." She put a hand on his arm. "Whatever you do don't rile him. You don't want his thugs on your tail."

"He won't do anything to me, Ruth. I'm family and, despite the violence, he's old school. Besides my mum would kill him."

Chapter 9

Tom Calladine couldn't remember when he'd last seen his cousin. But whenever it was, it wouldn't have been from choice, of that he was sure.

After circling the hospital car park for what seemed an age he finally found a spot, paid what seemed to him an exorbitant fee, and went to find the coronary care unit.

Ray Fallon was in a side room, with two uniformed constables standing guard outside. He lay in bed propped up on a pile of pillows, with an oxygen mask clamped to his face. He didn't look good. He was grey faced, and looked thinner and older than Calladine remembered.

As the detective entered the small room a bulky, dark-suited figure with a shaven head and clenched fists by his sides, rose from the bedside chair.

"It's okay, Donald. Thomas is family," Fallon told him.

"Thomas, good to see you." Fallon extended a hand, which Calladine ignored. "Go get some tea, Donald. I want to chat with my cousin."

"Bad do then." Calladine pulled up a chair and sat down. All the machinery surrounding the sick man made him nervous. "Will you be okay?"

"Now come on Thomas, I know you better than that. You don't really give a toss whether I live or die, do you? But from a copper's point of view, I suppose dead's better."

"Don't be so quick to judge, Ray. It's like you say — family — and my mum will want to know how you are."

"How is Auntie Freda? Hope you're doing a good job of looking after her. How old is she now? Must be in her mid-eighties I reckon."

"She's in a home. She got too much to cope with — dementia."

"How very disappointing, Thomas; I expected more of you — Leesdon's favourite son," he sneered. "You who promised to do so much, as I recall."

"We were kids. Reality's very different."

"Come off it. You've never had time for anything other than that job of yours. You had no time for your mother in the past, and I expect you've even less time for her now she's old. As I remember it, you had no time for that pretty wife of yours either. You're a first class loser, Thomas. Where family and women are concerned, you just can't cut it."

Fallon started to cough and leaned forward clutching his ribs. He was struggling to get his breath.

"You okay? Want the nurse?" asked Calladine.

"No — I'm fine. Just say whatever it is that brought you here, then fuck off."

Some things never changed. Heart surgery evidently hadn't softened Fallon any.

"You haven't come here for idle chitchat, Thomas. Come on, out with it. What is it you really want?"

Fallon was the only person he knew who used his full name — another source of irritation.

"The Hobfield Estate . . ."

Ray Fallon screwed up his eyes and shook his head.

"Don't give me any rubbish about not knowing the place, Ray, because I know you do. I also know that you run most of the dealers there."

"All the dealers, Thomas; not most of them. I hope you haven't come here because now I'm ill you think I'm a soft touch. A blabbermouth who'll just roll over and tell you everything." He laughed. It contained no humour, and made him cough again.

"Ice is dead, and so is Gavin Hurst." Calladine watched his cousin's face, and he saw that this was news to him. So not Fallon then. The visit had been worth it, just to see that look. "They've both been murdered, and I want to know why."

Fallon laughed again, and this time it held genuine mirth. "Not me, cousin. Definitely not me. I mean, look at me. I have neither the strength nor the inclination. Do you think I'd be stupid enough to get rid of a couple of cash cows like them? Those two were born to the job. They sell everything they can get their grubby little mitts on. They keep order among the customers, and they do a bloody good job of seeing off potential takeovers. So no, not me, not this time."

"They used to do all that, Ray. They're dead now, remember? So they can't work for you anymore. So who hated them — or you — enough to chop them both into little pieces and spread them around Leesdon?"

Fallon's eyes narrowed. "Now I know you're losing it, Inspector. Not my style. Never has been, as well you know. If I want rid of someone, they stay gone. They don't turn up dead in bits. They don't turn up at all."

That much was true. Fallon had made many enemies down the years, and used death as the ultimate punishment, but even he had never resorted to the barbarity Calladine had witnessed in the last few days.

Fallon leaned back on the pillows and closed his eyes. He'd had enough. His breathing had become laboured again and he was obviously tired. Calladine reached over and replaced the mask over his nose and mouth.

"Believe it or not, Ray, but talking to you today has helped with the case I'm working on. I hope you do pull through, despite everything."

Fallon raised an arm, a wave of sorts, but he didn't have the breath left to speak. As Calladine left the room, the goon returned with tea. He scowled at the policeman and banged the door shut after him.

* * *

Ruth Bayliss didn't know Leesworth Comprehensive from having attended it. She'd been lucky enough to win a place at a far more prestigious school in a neighbouring borough. But her brother had come here, so she knew it. The fabric of the place hadn't improved. It was still run down, with dirt-encrusted flooring and peeling paint on the corridor walls. The supposedly temporary portakabin classrooms still lurked in the playground. The place looked depressing at any time, but today, in the rain, it was horrendous.

She'd made an appointment to see the head, a Mr Deacon. He'd been here since the early nineties so, potentially, he should be helpful.

"I do remember the two boys, Ian Edwards and Gavin Hurst."

He sat behind his desk and waited, his fingers steepled into an arch in front of him. He couldn't be far off retirement, and looked worn down, a bit like the school itself. He was wearing shiny slacks and a shabby blazer. Not what Ruth expected of a headmaster.

"Do you recall the incident with David Morpeth, the lad who died here?"

Ruth didn't really see how anyone could forget something like that — not unless they had something to hide.

"Yes I do. It was only seven years ago."

"How does something like that happen? I mean —
for one of your pupils to end up dead, something must be
very wrong, surely."

"You have to understand, Sergeant Bayliss; this is a
difficult school. It doesn't do to stand out, to be in any
way different."

"Was that it — was David different? Did he stand
out?"

"He had Asperger Syndrome, a form of autism."

"Yes I know what it is. But I still don't understand
how that meant he ended up dead."

"It made him very uncommunicative. He wouldn't
speak to the other pupils, and he wouldn't make friends.
But the real problem was, he wouldn't react when he was
made fun of, or bullied. Or his reaction would be way over
the top. It made things worse."

"Didn't you try to stop it, the bullying I mean? Don't
you have a duty to look after your pupils, and particularly
those with special needs like David?"

"There is only so much we can do, Sergeant." His sigh
hinted at years of trying — and failing. "David did have a
defence mechanism. He had a spiteful streak. He could be
very vindictive himself when it suited."

"Do you mean to say that the incident was partly his
fault?"

"I don't know if it was or wasn't. All I know for sure
is that he was found at the bottom of the first floor
staircase, with head injuries."

"So where do Edwards and Hurst figure in this?"

"Because, when he was found, Hurst was bending
over the body and Edwards was walking down the stairs.
He was hooting and yelling — shouting how he'd done for
the bastard at last. His words not mine, Sergeant," he
added quickly. "But there was no evidence. No fresh
bruises to prove he'd been pushed, no witnesses, nothing
to implicate either boy."

"They were both interviewed, though. I've seen the records."

"Yes they were, but with no evidence it never went to court. So that was that. There was nothing more to be done."

"What sort of a boy was David? Did he have friends or siblings here?"

"No friends; the Aspergers saw to that. He swore a lot and spat if he didn't like what was said to him. Siblings . . ." He sat thoughtfully for a few seconds. "You see, the problem was that David was in foster care. We were told that his mother couldn't cope." He rolled his eyes in a derogatory fashion. "They don't try hard enough if you ask me. We get no end of kids from one parent families coming out of that dreadful estate. Most seem to manage after a fashion, but not David's mother apparently. I don't think there was anyone else."

Ruth decided she'd check with Social Services anyway. This man was a prat. It was obvious to Ruth that he'd either been in the job too long, or he wasn't cut out for it. He had no sympathy, no compassion for the kids in his care. With a man like him at the helm she could understand only too well why this place was the pits.

Before she left, Ruth popped her head round the staffroom door. "Detective Sergeant Bayliss," she announced to the two or three teachers taking a quick break from the fray. "I've been speaking to Mr Deacon about an incident that happened here a few years ago. Before I leave I wondered if any of you could help."

"Cold case, is that it?" A young man looked up from his marking.

"No, I'm actually investigating a current case." She smiled at him as she flashed her badge. "The old incident I'm on about is more in the nature of background."

"That would be the Morpeth boy, then?" A voice called from the back of the room. "I always knew that would rear its ugly head again. Those bastards might have got away with it at the time but they didn't fool me."

She was in luck.

"You were here then, sir?" Ruth took out her notebook.

"Yep, I most certainly was, and more to the point I was one of the first on the scene. I did give a statement at the time — it's all in there."

"I've still to look at the paperwork, but I'd like to speak to you, if you don't mind."

"Okay, I've got a little while before my next class."

"Why don't you think it was an accident?"

"Accident my . . . eye. Guilty as sin, the pair of them; but they were clever, played the innocent. You do know who I'm talking about, don't you. Bloody Edwards and Hurst — a pair of murdering tearaways who played the system and damn well got away with it. You've no idea what it was like seeing that poor boy lying there, dying. He was at the foot of the staircase and from the severity of the injury to his head, it was assumed he must have gone headlong down the entire flight."

"And you are?"

"Jake Ireson, Head of English." The man extended his hand.

He was nice; pleasant-looking with dark hair that was worn a little long. His brown eyes crinkled at the sides when he smiled and he had a slight tan. Perhaps he'd been away during half term. He looked like the type of man born to the job; safe, not too trendy. He was even wearing a tweed jacket — which almost made Ruth giggle. Ruth could imagine him teaching English and loving it, poring over Shakespeare with his class. No doubt making them all fall in love with it too.

"I'm making coffee. Want some?"

"That would be nice, thanks."

"Take a seat. Make yourself comfortable."

"So you still think it was deliberate, even after all this time?"

"I certainly do. Those two were evil then and things haven't changed since. They've got worse in fact. These days they are responsible for all the drug dealing we have to cope with. You should see what goes on outside the school gates over the average lunchtime — packages and cash changing hands second by second. The pair of them are rotten to the core. You've no idea what they put the poor Morpeth boy through, no one has. He never told anybody; he couldn't you see. He had problems speaking. And they were persistent little devils; every day they went at him with their taunts and bullying. And I mean real bullying. I saw the bruises."

"They've both been murdered, Mr Ireson. Edwards and Hurst have both been found dead in quite dreadful circumstances. That's what I'm investigating. I'm not here to re-examine the circumstances of David Morpeth's death. I'm trying to build a picture of them both, of how they operated. I'm trying to understand what would motivate someone to do what they did to them."

"Murdered! I don't know what to say. Probably no more than they deserve. Part of me is sorry, of course — they were both pupils of mine. I was their year group tutor and got to know them both well. But murder . . . that's a bit extreme."

"The way they were killed was certainly that, Mr Ireson. So you see I'm interested in any background information I can get. We are pursuing a number of enquiries but nothing concrete, not yet."

He grinned. "Is that a euphemism for you haven't got a clue?"

"No — it's exactly what I said; nothing concrete.

He handed her a mug of coffee and pointed to a battered old sofa. "Sit down, and I'll have a think. You see, the problem is that it's a while ago since the Morpeth boy, and I could do with mulling it over. As I said, I made a statement at the time so you can read that, but basically I got to the scene too late. Morpeth was already dead and no one had actually seen him fall. Edwards and Hurst were there, of course, ogling the scene and pretending to be shocked. But they weren't. It didn't touch them — hard bastards."

"Take your time, Mr Ireson. I'm interested in things around the incident, like family ties and friends we might not know about. A statement tends to contain only the bare facts, so I'd like a little more meat on the bone."

"I see. I'd like to help, to remember anything I can that might prove useful." He sat down beside her. "You think there's a link to what happened to them? Something that connects the two events?"

"I can't say yet. Not until I know more. But probably not. The incident with the Morpeth boy is just further proof of how wicked the two of them really were, and how adept they were at covering their tracks. But they certainly fell foul of someone recently who had the means to make them pay, and pay dear."

"It was her I felt sorry for — his mother. Poor cow, she stood no chance. She'd failed, you see. She couldn't cope with David and had to put him into care. She disappeared after his death. As far as I know, she left the area."

He took the empty mug from her hands and put it in the small sink in the corner of the room. He was nice, Ruth thought. Easy to speak to and quite good-looking. His hair wasn't only longish, but slightly spiky too. The more she looked at him, the more Ruth realised that he was a man she could fancy. He had his own little corner of the staff room full of his books. He obviously loved his work. Something they had in common.

"Look, I don't want this to sound too forward, but can we meet sometime, when I've had time to think about this some more?" he asked.

Even better! Ruth couldn't recall the last time a man had asked her out — if that's what this was.

"We could get together at the weekend perhaps — have something to eat and a drink. In the meantime I'll rack my brain, go back over the school records, look at some faces, and then I can give you a better overview of what happened. What do you say?"

Ruth raised her eyebrows. "Are you asking me out, Mr Ireson?"

He shrugged and buried his face in his coffee mug. "Suppose I am . . . Is that okay with you, Sergeant?"

Ruth nodded. Yes it certainly was . . . though against regulations, but she knew plenty of male officers who met women, while on the job.

Chapter 10

"DCI Jones is looking for you, and Doctor Hoyle's rung." Rocky said the moment Calladine entered the incident room.

That was good — well, the doc part was. He wasn't so keen on talking to Jones. He'd gone ahead and visited Fallon without his say-so. But that was only because Jones was too pedantic. If he'd waited for permission it would have been Christmas before he got clearance to speak to his cousin.

The case couldn't wait. They needed to make some headway, and fast. Hopefully there would something from the post-mortems. He could do with a break. He stared at the board. The faces, the images — they weren't talking to him. He couldn't get a handle on this at all. They were looking at murder — more than one, possibly serial murder. But why? What was the motive? He could understand why Edwards and Hurst weren't popular, but on the Hobfield they were vital. They were part of the very fabric of the place. Now they were gone a very real gap would have opened up. Who'd take over the business, who'd sell the dope? Perhaps he should have asked Ray Fallon.

"I've got a date," Ruth announced on her return. "Don't look at me like that . . ." Calladine's head had shot up and he gave her a questioning stare. "It does happen, you know. A sort of dishy teacher is taking me out to eat at the weekend."

"Only *sort* of dishy? Are you slipping?"

"Okay then — a *really* dishy teacher is taking me out. This is the first date I've had in ages, so I think I would have accepted no matter what. With my track record I can hardly afford to be too choosey. I'm a lot like you — no damn time for relationships."

"Well, have a nice time. But don't stay out too late, we've a lot on, remember?"

"It's a date but it's work related. He could be helpful. He was at the comp. when David Morpeth was killed, and he taught those two." She nodded at the board. "If nothing else, it's a different slant on their lives."

"In that case don't tell me anymore," he advised. "If it does turn out that your teacher knows something then he could be called as a witness once this little lot comes to court," he shook his head. "You can imagine what the defence would do with the knowledge that the pair of you were embroiled in some hot romance."

"It's not a *hot romance*, as you put it. I hardly know the guy," she frowned. "Wish I hadn't said anything now," she decided looking almost petulant.

"The way the case is going Ruth, so do I. So don't tell me anything else."

Calladine doubted anything from so far back would help and legal issues aside, he was glad Ruth was getting out. She tended to bury herself in her work, very much like he did, and this place could get claustrophobic if you didn't dip into the normal world every now and then.

"Bought Monika's present yet? Because if you haven't, you're leaving it very late. If you don't get a move on, it'll have to be flowers after all, and she'll know, she'll see right through you."

Calladine coughed. She had him there. He'd forgotten all about it — again. This damned romance business was too difficult. He had a job to do, and it didn't leave time to go bloody shopping.

"Doc Hoyle has something. I'll give him a ring." He retreated into his office.

He couldn't keep doing this, letting Monika down — not really caring. She was a problem he didn't want to face right now, but he'd have to come clean at some point. He'd get that present, he'd take her out, and once he'd got on top of this case and it wasn't her birthday, he'd speak to her properly.

"Doc, what've you got?"

"I've run some initial toxicology tests and got a whole mishmash of results. Both young men were full of Lorazepam. In large doses it's a sedative and can, in sufficient quantity, induce coma. But there were traces of other drugs too, and they are more perplexing."

"How do you mean? What did you find?"

"Risedronate for a start. I didn't expect that, it's usually prescribed for women suffering from osteoporosis. It would have no sedative effect at all. There was also Tramadol, a strong morphine-based painkiller, and then there was the real mystery."

There was a pause. Calladine could picture the man studying his notes and adjusting his reading spectacles.

"Aricept, Tom. A rather expensive drug used in the treatment of Alzheimer's."

"Is it a sedative?"

"No, not at all. The only two sedatives would be the Lorazepam and the Tramadol, and they are commonly prescribed by GPs."

"So why the other two then?"

"I can't even hazard a guess. Nor can I suggest where your murderer got the drugs from. Commonly used or not, they're all only issued on prescription. Unless, of course, they were bought online. But that still doesn't explain the choice."

"Thanks, Doc. Anything on the time of death, or how they died?"

"Difficult, but they've both been frozen at some time." He cleared his throat. "Unpalatable as it sounds, they were cut up and frozen in the plastic bags that were found around the scene."

"Method?"

"Stabbing, blow to the head, drugged . . . Given the state of the bodies it could be anything; so take your pick. I did find very fine slivers of metal from the implement used for the dismemberment. I've got Julian looking at them, so he may be able to tell you what was used."

"Good work. If anything else comes to light, let me know straight away."

Calladine went back into the incident room and wrote the names of the drugs on the board. This was something they could get their teeth into. It shouldn't take long to get a list of local people who'd been prescribed this little lot.

"Gather round folks! Before we call it a day, I've got something for you all to think about." He tapped the board. "Take a good look at this list of drugs. I want to know who, when and why. Speak to the local GP surgery. I'm told Lorazepam and Tramadol have a sedative effect but the other two . . ." He shook his head. "Doc Hoyle has no idea why our man would use them. That could be to our advantage. The Aricept is expensive and used to treat Alzheimer's. That might give us something."

"Does that mean we're looking for some off-his-head OAP?" Rocco smiled. "Looks like that from the list."

A ripple of laughter went around the room, until they caught sight of Calladine's unsmiling countenance.

"We're two days in, and no closer. I know this isn't drugs-related, so no turf war."

"How can you be sure, sir?" Dodgy asked. "Those drugs, it's the kind of thing a stupid kid, who knew no better, would dish out. It might be a case of the more pills he gets down them the better, regardless of what they are."

That would explain the strange concoction of drugs, but Calladine had spoken to Fallon. So it wasn't that simple. Whatever the reason for the pills, it wasn't about some kid using anything he could get his hands on.

"Julian is analysing the plastic bags. Fragments of metal were found on the bodies, so we might learn something about the implements that were used. Oh — and they'd both been frozen prior to dumping. That signifies a large freezer. In fact this entire thing required plenty of space and no interruptions. So it's safe to presume we're not looking at a flat on the Hobfield, not with their tacky construction. And it's another reason I don't think this is drugs related. The only places the crew on the estate have got is their own flats. There's little or no privacy. So we need to look further afield."

The pills, a breakthrough of sorts, presented them with another problem. There was only one GP practice in Leesworth and it had thousands of patients. Then there was the walk-in centre on the outskirts of Oldston that folk used out of hours, plus the ED at the hospital. The Aricept was their best bet.

"Message for you, sir," called out Joyce as he made his way back to the quiet of his office. "There's a woman waiting to see you downstairs. She asked for you by name, says she has some information."

Ruth looked up from her desk. "Want me to come; another pair of ears?"

"No, it's okay. You get on. We need to make some headway on this. But you could give whoever's watching Kelly Griggs's flat a ring and see if she's turned up yet."

Calladine pulled on his suit jacket as he bounded down the stairs to the reception area. A uniformed police officer was dealing with an irate man, who sounded drunk — trying to point out that it wasn't police responsibility to dictate when the local shops closed.

"Miss Holden! I intend to arrange a press briefing for some time in the next two days. So I still can't tell you much I'm afraid."

"That's okay, Inspector." She smiled. "I've told you before — call me Lydia. This time I've got some information for you." She held up what looked like the front page of the following day's *Leesworth Echo*.

What Calladine saw made his blood run cold. She had it all: their names, every gory detail, from the severed digits to the remains left strewn across the common, as well as a description of the mark left behind by the perpetrator. Not only that, the newspaper had given him a name. It was the headline for the piece she'd written.

Handy Man.

Calladine shook his head in disbelief. "You can't print that!" "Why not, Inspector? It's all true, you know it is. I got this first-hand, excuse the pun."

"What do you mean? Where did you get this? Who gave you this information?"

What Lydia Holden had done with the information was shocking. Surely she wouldn't jeopardise the case by flaunting that — that horror — in front of the public. Leesworth would be in turmoil. There'd be panic and mayhem. "I got it from the man himself. Well, I presume it was him. It came via email. To my email address at the newspaper this morning, along with a snippet of film you might find interesting."

"You can't print it. You can't let that go out."

She was looking at him with a smug expression on her pretty face. The sort of expression he'd seen women use when they knew they had the upper hand and intended to use it.

What the hell was going on? This wasn't the usual behaviour of murderers. They usually craved anonymity, at least if they expected to get away with it. They certainly didn't broadcast their misdemeanours to the press in glorious Technicolor!

"Calm down, Tom. I can call you Tom, can't I?"

Her blue eyes were sparking with mischief. She watched him, the puzzlement in his eyes. How his expression softened slightly. Yes, she had him on the run. She ran a hand through her blonde hair, fluffing it over her shoulders.

"Yes. But you still can't publish that."

"I don't intend to," she admitted. "See, this is a mock-up of what I could do. I don't want you under any illusions, Detective. I want this story. I want access to all the details the minute you are free to release them. This is a big deal for me, and probably for you too. Tell me, Tom, when was the last time you had a serial killer in your sights? I've never reported a case like this before, and I don't intend to mess it up, because it could be my ticket to bigger things."

"We don't know he is a serial killer, not yet. He might just have wanted to rid the world of those two."

"We'll see. We have to hope there are no more, but I bet you don't believe there won't be. Now, do you want to see this film?" She smiled, and handed him the sheet of newsprint. "Shall I come up to your office, and I'll access it from your computer?"

"Yes, yes, come up." What was the use? She was going to get her own way regardless.

He'd take her into his office, but he didn't want her seeing the incident board. But then again — she knew everything they did anyway. She had it all neatly packaged on that damned front page.

But why tell the press? And more particularly, why her? If their man wanted the police to know, then why not just tell him? It had to be the publicity. Whatever information Lydia Holden had, it wouldn't help the case, he realised. The killer would have given her no more than they already knew — which wasn't much. But he'd be hoping the gory detail would carry the story.

"Show me." Calladine had seated the reporter in front of his PC.

Lydia tapped away for a few seconds, and then leaned back, allowing him to look at the long list of emails.

She opened one of them.

What Calladine read made his flesh crawl. It was all there. No embellishments. The names, the brutality, and where he'd left the body parts. But there were no clues as to who he might be, or where all this had taken place.

"And the film?"

She clicked on a link. "It doesn't make good viewing, believe me, Tom. It's horrific, but fortunately the youth is unconscious throughout."

The film was very dark and shaky, but the cutting of the fingers could be seen clearly enough. Each cut was made with what looked like a pair of secateurs, and the digits were left to drop onto the dirty floor.

"Forward the email to me. I'll get my people on it straight away."

He knocked on the partition window between his office and the incident room and beckoned Ruth to join them.

"This is Lydia Holden from the *Leesworth Echo*. I don't think you two have been formally introduced. Ruth Bayliss is my sergeant. We work closely together, so anything you divulge to me will be passed on to her."

Ruth smiled and nodded at the woman. Calladine could see her clocking the reporter's expensive clothes and designer handbag. Lydia was lithe, tall and had gorgeous hair. Ruth wasn't bad-looking or overweight — well not much — but she was probably borderline, and the clothes she wore did nothing to hide it.

"Watch this," Calladine instructed. "It's definitely X-certificate I'm afraid; very much so."

Minutes later a much paler Ruth pushed the chair back from the desk.

"We need to know where this came from, Ruth. I'll forward it to you, then you can show it to Imogen."

"What we get will depend on how much the sender wants to hide. But between Imogen and our IT people, we'll give it a go."

Calladine forwarded the email and then watched the gruesome clip once again.

"I'll get this cleaned up. We might see or hear something we can use."

"I'll forward it to the lab."

Ruth made her way back to her desk in the incident room. Imogen had left, so there was no one to share the new information with.

"I'd say I'd done you one very big favour, Detective." Lydia gave him one of her devastating smiles. "I think I deserve a little reward, don't you?"

She was flirting. Calladine could hardly believe it, but she really was. What was going on? What could this lovely young woman want with him, an aging detective with relationship issues? He sighed. Who was he kidding? It was all about keeping up with the case. She'd already said it was important to her, and she couldn't risk missing anything. She was going use him, and she was being blatant about it too.

"What sort of reward?"

"Well, we can start with dinner. You can come round to my apartment later and I'll cook something. We don't have to talk about this . . ." She waved a manicured hand. "I know it bothers you, but sooner or later you are going to have to talk to me. So we need to strike up some sort of relationship, don't we, Detective? And I for one would prefer it was friendly." She handed him her card. "That's my personal card, the one with my private number and address on it. I'll expect you at eight."

"We'll eat. But I won't change my mind about the case, and you need to understand that from the outset. I won't be cajoled, or bribed or backed into a corner." He looked down at the front page mock-up he still held in one hand. "I'll need to keep this. You've captured the essence of that email very well. 'Handy Man.' Is that yours? Did you come up with that apt little title?"

"No, not me. He did. It's how he signed off the email, didn't you see?"

Chapter 11

Malcolm Masheda held her close. It was dark in the alley that led to the side entrance of his block, and he'd chosen this spot deliberately.

"You could come up with me, babe," he told Cuba, as he fitted her with one of the earbuds from his mobile so that she could share his music. "My ma will go apeshit if I'm late."

"Damned tag — you should get it fixed." She pulled out the earbud and poked his chest in annoyance. "You're a good boy. Tell them you've changed; you've done the Community Service. Be a man, Mash, and stand up for your rights and get them to take it off."

"I can't. My ma says I got to wait until they say." He wanted to make Cuba happy. He loved her, but his mother wasn't keen on the girl, and the rule that he had to be back under her roof by seven thirty, suited her just fine.

"I have to live up there, with her. I have to do what she wants. It's her place anyway. If I don't do what she says, then she'll throw me out. So for now I've got to live with this." He flashed the tag attached to his leg. "I have to stay at home. It's part of the deal, and anyway I don't want to doss down on the deck. I'll get a kicking."

"Gangs." Cuba spat. "I hate this place and everyone in it. We can do better. We should leave here, now, tonight. Together." She drew her head back and looked him straight in the eye. "What about it?" Her hands rested on her slim hips. "Are you up for it? Will you man up and break away with me?"

Mash tried to laugh off her idea. But he knew from the look in her dark eyes that she meant it. His head and shoulders drooped. "I can't."

He had to try and make it right. He wanted Cuba to be okay with what they had. For the time being, at least, it was all he could do. He kissed her hard.

"You're a disgrace," she fired at him, once they'd separated. "You got no balls, bad boy." With a smirk, she reached between his thighs.

"Aw, man, don't!"

"We could go, you know. You can get that thing removed if you want to. You know people, just like I do, who'll do it for nothing."

"I'm trying to be different. It was you said you wanted that. This place, this life, it's no good. Things need to change and this is the first step." He pulled her towards him again.

"You're so wrong, Mash. You're wrong to stay and take it and you'll pay. You'll be made to pay. The others won't let you change, you know that."

They were so wrapped up in their argument that neither of them heard the footsteps. They didn't notice a third presence looming close in the dark. The quiet, purposeful footsteps edged closer; the man was pressed against the wall of the block. Mash was momentarily aware of the tall shadow on the wall beside them. He didn't hear the click of the gun or the dull thud as the bullet entered Cuba's back. Mash only realised something had happened when Cuba went limp in his arms.

His grip on her body slackened, and she slithered to the floor like a rag doll. He saw that his hands were covered in her blood. He stared at them in disbelief. He looked around. Cuba was down on the cold concrete, still and bleeding; he had to help her. He knelt down, but she didn't move. He moved his head close to her chest. Was she breathing? He couldn't tell; his own heart was beating far too loud. There was another dull thud. Searing pain. Then everything went black.

* * *

"Detective! Welcome." Lydia Holden held open the door.

"You found me, then. You can park at the back."

"I got a taxi. Thought there might be drink involved?" The truth was he'd thought about more than just the drink. Calladine had agonised about coming here tonight. He was doing exactly what Ruth was doing — fraternising with a possible witness, and one from the press at that. What was wrong with him — he knew the rules? If Jones got wind of this he'd throw the book at him.

"I was hoping you'd come. I would have been terribly disappointed if you'd cried off." She rubbed his cheek gently with her hand. "You look wonderful. A veritable feast of maleness."

Calladine wasn't sure what to make of that. For someone who was simply interested in getting a story, she was going to a lot of trouble. Perhaps he shouldn't analyse it too much — gift horses and all that. It was just one of those things. It was possible that she did find him attractive — younger women did go for older men — quite often, in fact. Nah, who was he kidding?

He followed her up a rather grand flight of stairs to her apartment on the first floor. She obviously lived in some style. The old mill building had been beautifully renovated. The newspaper business must pay better than he thought.

"I nearly didn't come tonight. I don't go out with women I don't know as a rule. I have someone in my life, and I'm not keen to upset things. And I have to ask myself why you'd be interested in me in the first place." There, he thought — get it straight from the beginning.

She laughed at that, and the sound echoed around the high ceilings like musical notes. "Oh, I think you do, Detective. You are a very desirable man. But I won't complicate anything. You're here tonight because I want to keep you close." She turned around and ran her manicured nails down his chest. "We'll eat, we'll talk — and then we'll see. I won't pick your brains. You don't have to tell me anything you don't want to, and I certainly won't force you. That's the deal — not too difficult."

Calladine cleared his throat. She made it all so sound so easy — too easy. This woman was young, very lovely, and obviously making a play for him. Was she offering him her body in exchange for information? A ridiculous idea that he dismissed almost as soon as it entered his head. But all the same, it left an uneasy feeling behind.

And she'd dressed to kill. She wore a skimpy, short-skirted number that emphasised her figure, and she teetered up the stairs on ultra-high heels. The sight of this beautiful woman reinforced his doubts. He shouldn't have come here at all. He shouldn't have fallen for it, this illusion she was spinning. He didn't know what had possessed him. He should be back at his own place, with Monika.

"It's small, it's different but it is all mine," she announced, as they entered her apartment.

Calladine had not been inside one of these places before, so he'd never seen what the developers had done with the old mill. But he was impressed. Lydia's apartment was open plan — not something that would suit him, too expensive to heat. The ceilings were high and many of the original features had been left behind. The old stone flags still lay on the floor. They'd been cleaned and varnished, but they were the ones that had seen hundreds of pairs of clogs trample over them across the decades. The ceiling was beamed and the dark oak stripped to make it lighter. Tall windows let in natural light that must fill the place during the daytime.

"It's been beautifully done. I knew this place as a lad when it was a working mill — not so lovely then, I promise you."

"I think it's great. This would cost a fortune in London, which is partly why I moved north." She poured two glasses of red wine. "I sold my tiny flat in Camden and could afford to buy this outright. Brilliant, don't you think? I can't understand why more folk don't do it."

"Work is what stops them. Jobs are not that plentiful up here — and then there's the weather." They both laughed at this.

"Yes, why is it so wet up here?"

"It's the hills, the Pennines. We sit in a little semi-circle of land with the hills all around. So the rain clouds get trapped. That's what my mum always used to tell me, anyway."

"Your mum, is she . . .?"

"She's still with us and doing okay. She lives in a care home, run by a good friend of mine."

He didn't want to say too much about Monika; it would only spoil the mood. What the hell was he thinking? He shouldn't be here, and he shouldn't be trying to hide the fact that Monika was a big part of his life.

"Perhaps I should go." He put his wine glass down on the table. "Frankly, I should never have come."

"Oh, don't spoil things now. Please stay. You're the first man I've met since I've been here, and, putting the case aside for a while, I would like to get to know you better." She put down her own wine glass and wrapped her arms around him. "Don't you want to get to know me a little better too? Don't you find me attractive, Detective?"

She planted little kisses on his cheek, slowly trailing them around to his mouth. "Kiss me, Tom. Kiss me hard."

The kiss was deep and sensual. Resistance and all thoughts of the case gone, moments later his jacket and tie hit the sofa and she dragged him off to her bedroom. A flurry of discarded clothing and flailing limbs, and then she was on top of him, her naked breasts brushing his chest hair.

Lydia Holden gave one of her dazzling smiles and produced a small foil packet from the bedside table. "Allow me, Detective." Moments later, she lowered her body onto his.

He sank gratefully into her welcoming warmth. She groaned with pleasure, swept back the curtain of long, blonde hair from her face and continued to rise and fall on his prone body. Lydia Holden was determined to make this a night he wouldn't forget in a hurry.

Chapter 12

Wednesday

By the time Calladine woke it was daylight. For a few desperate seconds he couldn't think where he was. And then it hit him. He'd spent the night with Lydia Holden — worse than that he'd spent a night of shameless debauchery with Lydia Holden. What on earth had possessed him? More to the point, what about Monika?

He groaned and rubbed a hand over his brow. He had one heck of a headache. Served him right, cheating bastard that he was. If Monika ever found out about this she'd never forgive him, and who could blame her?

The soft female hand rested on his arm. Lydia lay with her eyes closed, breathing regularly, with a small smile on those luscious, expert lips of hers. Oh God, how he'd enjoyed this woman!

He checked his watch and found he'd overslept. He'd have to re-live the delights of Lydia Holden's body later. The rest of his team would be hard at it by now. He pushed things around on the bedside table, but he couldn't find his mobile. It must still be in his jacket pocket.

He crept out of her bed as quietly as he could manage, but heard her groan. He watched as she ran her hand over the bed sheet where he'd just been lying.

"Tom, don't go, it's early." She rose onto her elbows to watch his naked figure tiptoeing through her bedroom door.

"Work, Lydia," he called back, scooping up his discarded clothing from the floor and retiring into her bathroom.

Ruth would be ringing round trying to find him. It was way past nine and he should have been at his desk over an hour ago. Ruth would want to know where he'd been. What was he going to tell her? Not the truth, that's for sure.

Calladine showered and dressed. There was no shaving gear in the bathroom, so he'd have to pass by his place once he'd checked in. For now he'd have to go with the rugged, stubbly look.

There were five missed calls from Ruth on his mobile. "Sorry, Ruth, my battery went dead," he lied. "Is something up?"

"Cuba Hassan was found last night on the estate — she's been shot. She was discovered in the narrow alley up the side of Heron House in the early hours. She was lucky to be found at all and she's in a bad way."

He groaned. He'd taken his eye off the ball for one night — one solitary night — and this happened.

"Malcolm Masheda?"

"We can't find him. His mother hasn't seen him since yesterday afternoon and doesn't know what he's been up to. She's just come back from Trinidad. She only flew in to Manchester yesterday morning."

"Is someone with Cuba at the hospital?"

"Her mother; and I've got a uniformed PC there. She's in intensive care, but it's been a good few hours since her op so she should be coming round soon."

"I'll meet you there. Damn, I've no car. I left it at home last night. Can you pick me up? I'll wait outside for you — in about five minutes. Okay?"

"Outside where, sir? Where are you?"

"Wrigley Mill Apartments in Hopecross."

Now he'd done it but he'd had no choice. Ruth would be intrigued, but it wouldn't take her long to work it out. She'd know her DI had been out and hadn't been home all night. She'd also know that it wasn't Monika who lived in one of those swanky apartments in that upmarket little village either. So she'd want to know what he'd been up to. Even more interesting, who had he been up to it with. She'd tear into him for letting Monika down. It was rare that he even spent the night at Monika's place. Dare he tell her the truth — admit who had tempted him away from his own fireplace at last? He'd see how things went.

After a brief explanation to Lydia, Calladine left the apartment and waited outside in the icy drizzle for Ruth to arrive. He'd not meant to stay the entire night — he'd not meant for things to go that far. A bite to eat, she'd said. He shook his head; they'd never even got as far as eating . . .

"I can take you in, Tom." There she was, emerging through the entrance doors in a designer suit and clutching a briefcase.

She looked lovely, and he felt suddenly tongue-tied. What was this damn woman doing to him?

"I'm practically passing the station, so it's no bother." She gave him one of her smiles, which he was sure could melt ice.

"Thanks, Lydia, but my sergeant's picking me up."

"We'll do this again, Detective." She said and kissed his cheek. "Next time you won't be so rude. You won't leave a girl lying in bed craving her breakfast treat." She smirked wickedly as she reached around him and squeezed his backside before teetering off in the rain.

As bad luck would have it, Ruth chose that very moment to pull up beside him and wind her car window down. "If I'm not mistaken that's the blonde bimbo from the Echo. She must really have something special, getting my guv to do the *walk of shame*," she teased, seeing that he was wearing his good suit and silk tie. "You've been out all night, haven't you? And not with Monika either. So come on, why that particular hottie? And don't lie, because if you do I'll tell, and Monika will be livid. In fact she'll be more than livid — she'll kill you."

He'd been caught red-handed. This was the plain-speaking version of Ruth giving him both barrels — but he probably deserved it.

"She asked me round, she's good company and I like her. Do we have time to call in at my place? I need a shave."

He didn't much like the look on Ruth's face. He knew that look and it always unnerved him. "And if you do tell Monika, I'll have you demoted, Sergeant. We both have a little secret to keep now, and that's how they should stay — secret."

Ruth grinned. "I never had you down as any sort of womaniser, Tom Calladine, and particularly not the type who'd attract someone like Lydia Holden. Not that you couldn't," she added hastily. "It's just that women like her tend to go for a different sort of man."

"What you mean is the younger sort."

"If you like," she smirked. "So in my book that means she's after something and you should be careful."

"Keep your opinions to yourself, Sergeant."

"In my opinion you seeing a reporter goes one better than my school teacher — what do you say? What if that little shocker reached the wrong ears? What if Jones got wind of it?"

She was joking, she had to be. Calladine's head shot round and he gave her a long hard look. There was a grin on her face — she had him banged to rights.

"Okay. I'll keep your dirty little secret — but because of Monika, not you. Understand?"

He nodded. He understood only too well.

* * *

Cuba Hassan lay in the intensive-care bed covered in what looked like tin foil and wired up to the machines that were monitoring her vital signs. The trace on the display seemed to wave about wildly, so much so that Calladine nudged the nurse and asked if that was her heart.

"Her breathing. She's actually doing okay at the moment. Her heart is strong, but one of her lungs was injured."

"The bullet nicked the lower lobe of the right lung, Detective Inspector." The doctor entered the room. "We've removed the bullet and passed it to your forensic team."

So Julian would be examining it right now — to find out whether it was a match for the bullet that had killed Richard Pope.

"We've been helping her with her breathing and slowly raising her core temperature. It was freezing last night, and she's got mild hypothermia."

Calladine turned to the tearful coffee-coloured woman at Cuba's bedside.

"Mrs Hassan—"

"It's Karen Miller. I was never Hassan. Bastard left as soon as we registered her, and I haven't seen him since."

He closed his eyes. Another example of typical family life on the Hobfield.

"When did you last see Cuba, Karen?"

"She came home to eat yesterday, about four in the afternoon. Mash came round an hour or so later and she left with him." She sobbed and clamped a tissue to her face. "They can't find him. The bastard has done this to my Cuba then done a runner."

"We don't know that, Karen. Mash and Cuba were close. I saw them together myself only yesterday. Mash is no angel, but this is way over the top even for a young man with his background."

"Come on, Inspector. He's a drug-dealing gang member with a reputation for violence. He's not the type you mess with and he's got a temper. He did for her, you'll see."

She wasn't entirely wrong, but Mash hadn't been in trouble for a while now. Tagged yes, but for a minor offence, not violence, and not drug dealing. But there was no way Karen Miller was going to believe that, not until Cuba regained consciousness and told her.

"Will she recover?" Calladine asked the doctor.

"I should think so. She was lucky, a fraction further to the left . . . if she hadn't been found, then it would be a very different story."

"See! He wanted to kill her. He wanted her dead." Karen was raving now. "What if he comes back? What if he tries again? What are you lot going to do to protect her?"

"We'll do our best to find Mash, don't worry. There'll be a police presence here all the time. She's quite safe."

Calladine could tell that she didn't believe anything he said. But instinct told him this wasn't down to Malcolm. He leaned over the girl. She was blinking her eyes, trying to open them. There was a sudden noise from one of the machines, and the doctor moved forward.

"What's happening? Is she alright?"

"I think she's coming round." Ruth took Karen's arm and helped her to her feet. "Stand back, let the doctor see her."

"Cuba? Can you hear me?" He pressed a stethoscope to her chest.

Cuba Hassan moaned and moved her lips. Her mouth was very dry and she coughed. Her eyes blinked in shock at all the people staring at her.

A nurse offered her a drink in a sort of baby beaker. She took a sip from it and licked her lips.

"Mash? Is he here?" Her voice was a whisper.

"Did he do this?" Her mother strained forward, shrugging Ruth's arm off her shoulder. "Did that moron do this to you?"

Cuba shook her head and screwed up her large brown eyes. "No. Mash wouldn't hurt me. I felt a burning, then nothing. He was kissing me, I was in his arms . . . he wouldn't do this."

Ruth turned to Calladine.

"So where is he, then? Why haven't we found him and why hasn't he come here to see Cuba?"

Calladine signalled for her to follow him out into the corridor. "We'll go and talk to Hoyle, see what he makes of this."

"You thinking what I'm thinking, boss?" He shivered. "I'm afraid so. He and Cuba were very close. He wouldn't leave her like that if he had any choice. I think our young Mr Masheda may well have met with his worst nightmare."

* * *

Doctor Hoyle could add nothing to dispel their fears.

"She was shot in the back from a few yards away. If she was in Masheda's arms then it wasn't him. Even if he reached around with the gun there'd be powder marks on her clothing and skin, and there are none."

"Looks like our man, then."

"I'm having the bullet checked, Tom. I shouldn't speculate, but it would help if it was a match for the one that killed Richard Pope. I'll keep you posted."

"Edwards and Hurst?"

Hoyle shook his head. "Dreadful mess. I'm still doing the DNA in order to match the right bits to the right body."

Ruth felt sick. She couldn't help picturing those two on trolleys, with Hoyle working on them as if they were a pair of jigsaws.

"Back to the nick, Ruth. Bring the team up to date and see if we can find Mash."

Their eyes met. Both knew that the next time they set eyes on Malcolm Masheda, they'd be lucky if they could even recognise him.

Chapter 13

He had a blinding headache and he was cold. Something awful had happened, but he couldn't remember what. He tried, racked his brain, but thinking was too painful.

"Mr Masheda! You're back."

He was being offered a drink. A cardboard beaker was put to his lips, and he took a large slurp of the cold fluid. Water? He thought so, but it was bitter tasting. Why couldn't he hold it himself? Mash tried to lift his arms and realised that he was bound tight to something.

"You'll feel better soon. Getting you here was easier than I thought." The voice chuckled. "You lot really are letting your guard down these days, aren't you?"

The water was taken away and a piece of cloth was pushed into his mouth. He couldn't speak and he didn't have the strength to push it out. What had happened to him? He couldn't see; wherever he was, it was dark.

Mash closed his eyes and tried to think. He'd been with Cuba. They'd been talking and listening to music. He'd been about to go home, to see his mother. Cuba had talked about going away. She wanted to be with him. A pulse of terror rushed through his body; a shock so fierce it made him tremble violently.

He'd been holding her, kissing her and then her blood was on his hands. How could that happen? Someone had hurt her, hurt her real bad and now they'd taken him. But what about Cuba? What had happened to her? He felt warm tears run down his cheeks, but he couldn't wipe them away. Cuba was dead, she must be. She'd looked so still.

"I'm sorry, Mash." His captor was speaking. "You don't mind me being so familiar, do you? I mean it isn't as if we know each other or anything, but I've heard of you, of course. Your reputation on the estate has gone before you."

Mash grunted behind the gag. He could call him whatever he wanted as long as he let him go.

"I'm sorry but I can't keep you here for very long, Mash. It just isn't practical. Now last month, last month I would have had all the time I needed. We could have spent time getting to know each other better, before . . . well, before you left me."

Did that mean he was going to let him go? Was this some elaborate tactic to frighten him? What about Cuba?

"You see I've got to get to work, and you're a loose end I don't want to leave behind."

Mash was shaking. If he got out of this, he would change. He'd do what Cuba wanted, he'd straighten himself out. She'd like that.

The man was walking about. Mash could hear his heavy boots clump on the hard floor.

"I do wish this could be different, I really do, but I just haven't got the time. I want my breakfast before I leave for the day job. You understand, don't you, Mash? Some of us have to work. Not all of us can spend our days lazing around the community centre, or wandering round the estate trying to make a buck. Some of us have rent and bills to pay. If only you'd made something of yourself, young man, this could all have been so very different."

Mash wanted to speak out in his defence, but the cloth in his mouth had become a hard, dry lump and was stuck to his teeth. He planned to change, he wanted to say, Cuba was sorting him out. Cuba. Was she really dead? He sobbed into the dark.

He felt a slight tickle. Something hard and cold travelled from his throat to his lower belly like an icy rivulet. It made the hairs on the back of his neck stand on end. His eyes searched the darkness. There was a white, shrouded figure in front of him, and the tickle suddenly came stronger, firmer.

"I think this will be quick, but if it isn't you'll have to forgive me. I've never disembowelled anyone before — not while they were breathing anyway."

Mash tried to scream. He was frantic. He did the best he could to open his mouth, but there was no sound. He struggled and pulled against the restraints and received a hard slap across his face with something cold and metallic. The blow was fierce enough to dislodge a tooth. He could feel it loose and bloody in his mouth. He wanted to spit it out, but he couldn't.

"Bye, bye, Mash. I'll call in later to make sure you've gone."

The blade went in somewhere between his ribs just above his stomach. It didn't go deep, just enough to open the skin and draw blood. Using two hands the man slowly dragged the blade down the youth's body, going in deeper as he got nearer to his navel and below.

He stood back, waiting, but there was nothing but stifled screaming and blood, lots of blood. He'd done it wrong. He threw the large blade to the floor angrily and picked up the more delicate paring knife. He took his torch and illuminated Mash's abdomen. He hadn't gone in far enough. He could plainly see the thin curtain of muscle, the mesentery, still holding the intestines in place. Using the finer blade he swiftly cut through the remaining tissues and with his gloved hands held the flesh apart. Now it began. He felt the youth's insides move.

Standing back he watched, intrigued, and with growing satisfaction as Malcolm Masheda's guts plopped onto the cold floor.

Chapter 14

"I want a heavy presence on the estate for the next few days. If by some chance Malcolm Masheda's still alive, then we need to find him. Talk to people — find out what he was doing last night, who saw him and Cuba. Talk to his mother, find out when he left the flat, and exactly when she saw him last."

Rocco's mouth wore a grim smile. "Still looks like drugs to me. The three main protagonists are gone; two we know are dead for sure. Someone's taking over — someone new, and he could even be hoping to oust Fallon now that he's in no state to run his empire."

Calladine knew this was wrong. He could see what it looked like, but it wasn't a takeover. And, fit or not, Fallon's grip on the area was as strong as it had ever been.

"Look at the information he's sent to the paper. Look at his methods. No. This is something else. No one would challenge Fallon in this way; they wouldn't dare."

Ruth spoke up, "We need to find something that links the lot of them. There's something else, apart from the obvious drugs thing. Perhaps something in their past."

"Like what?" Dodgy asked. "This crew has spent their entire lives together, living on that estate, going to the same school. There's lots of stuff that links them, so how do we find whatever's relevant?"

"We dig," Ruth answered. "We look at all three and go back as far as it takes until we find something."

"I've been all through the CCTV, sir," Imogen piped up. "And some from weeks ago that the off licence gave us. Those three didn't even hang out together. Mash spent all his time with Cuba."

"Okay. Leave that for now. Spend your time on the email and cleaning up the film. We need to know where it came from — narrow down the area if possible."

"I did ask the IT team at Central, in Manchester, for some help but they're chocker with their own stuff so I've got it earmarked as my next priority."

"Kelly Griggs? Anyone seen her yet?"

"We're still watching out for her. Rumour has it she's gone away for a few days, her and the babe," Rocco told them.

"How does Kelly afford to go anywhere?" Ruth asked. "She lives hand to mouth. She's no family to bung her the cash, so where's she got the money from?"

"Well she can't stay away forever, so once she's back; bring her in for a chat."

He wrote the three names on the incident board, inside a circle. Ice, Gavin and Mash. Outside the circle he wrote 'Cuba' and 'Richard Pope'.

"Something ties these five together. It's probable that Cuba simply got in the way when Mash was being taken. But we can't say that about Richard, can we? Julian is examining the bullets; if they're a match, then we have one shooter — one gun — but still no idea what the hell's going on."

"Tom!" DCI Jones had spotted a lull in the briefing. "Can I have a word when you're done?"

"Dodgy, get a list of people taking those drugs; the Aricept particularly. When I've done with Jones, Ruth and

I will go back to the Hobfield. Get to it, folks, we'll convene later with what we've got."

Calladine grabbed his suit jacket and went into Jones's office.

"I specifically asked you to wait for my say-so before you saw Fallon. It's not good enough, Tom. You can't just go off on a whim, regardless of your special circumstances."

"Sorry, George, but it was vital I spoke to him. The way forward with this case hinged on what I got from him."

"And what was that?"

"He didn't know about the murders. Whatever's going on had nothing to do with him."

"And you believe that?" Jones was astonished. "Because I certainly don't. For a start it hasn't taken him long to replace that pair . . . There're already two new dealers making their presence known on the estate. Rumour is that Fallon appointed them himself, and they've got one of his flats in Heron House. How does that work, Tom?" Jones asked with genuine puzzlement. "That entire estate is made up of social-housing stock, so how come Fallon is able to allocate flats the way he does?"

Calladine hid a smirk and shook his head. "Because he's a *hard bastard* and no one dares cross him. He'll have turfed the previous occupant out on their ear."

"We should bring him in. Teach him not to be so damned sure of himself."

"But we can't, can we, sir? Because he's already in custody, well hospital, recovering from lifesaving surgery. And even if we could we'd be stepping on toes, and Fallon would only retaliate. Not something we need right now."

"Here's the address. There are two youths and their mother living there. The Foxleys: Liam and Josh. Bring them in asap. What we need is an end to this bloody shambles. No more messing around, use Long's team for the legwork. Get them to look at all that CCTV if you

117

must. Never mind your finer feelings or your damned instincts; get this moving, Tom. Stop pissing about with wild theories. I want it sorted by the end of the week."

The DCI was obviously getting flak from above. He was trying to walk that narrow line between keeping faith with the teams and pleasing management. Not an enviable position

"With respect, sir, they're all the wrong moves. I'm certain this isn't down to Fallon or about drugs. If it was any sort of takeover there'd have been a whole barrowload of trouble, and that hasn't happened. Most of the estate doesn't even know about any of it yet. This is about something else, but I've no idea what."

Why couldn't Jones see what was staring him in the face? Why did he persist in going down this dead end?

"Well it's plain enough to the rest of us. Masheda shot the girl, so it's a long way from finished. Get out there, Tom. Bring in Masheda and the Foxleys and you'll have your culprits. This isn't difficult at all. It makes perfect sense. Some bright spark fancied his chances and has tried to scare Fallon with these gruesome tactics. Fallon's ill. For all we know he's scared too and so he's rolled over and let them in."

Calladine bit his lip. Fallon scared! He doubted he even knew the meaning of the word. If he said what was on his mind, it might just finish him. Jones was an idiot, a bloody fool, if he really thought this was so simple.

"With respect again, sir. You're wrong. Masheda's been taken and I bet he's already dead."

"Bet! Think! Admit it, Tom, you're flailing around in the bloody dark and dragging your team along behind you. It isn't good enough. Look at the evidence, look at what's staring you full in the face, for goodness' sake."

"The evidence doesn't point either way, but I've spoken to Fallon, remember."

He was trying to keep his cool. He mustn't lose his temper with the DCI.

"Oh, and he's a paragon of law and order, isn't he? He's lying through his eye teeth. He'd tell you anything and, like a fool, you'd swallow it!"

"It's not like that between Fallon and me, sir. We don't get on. But I still don't believe he's lying. Ice and Gavin did a good job for him. If someone had ousted them, then Fallon would be the first to complain. And that doesn't explain Mash; he wasn't on Fallon's payroll, remember?"

"Then he must have got in the way somehow, him and the girl. Go and get them, Tom. Go and find that gun, all the evidence you need, and wrap this up."

It was no use arguing with him. Jones had it sorted and that was that. Calladine went back to the incident room.

"Ruth and Rocco — with me," he barked. "The rest of you get on with finding me some names to go with those drugs. If Doc Hoyle rings or Kelly Griggs turns up, then ring me straight away."

"Where are we going, sir?" Ruth hurried along in his wake.

"The Hobfield, to bring in the two new boys. The DCI thinks the Foxley brothers are responsible for the bloody lot of it. So I don't have much choice but to agree and do as he wants — for now anyway."

"We don't know that pair, sir. We could be walking into anything. If it is them, then we know they've got guns."

"Worry not, Rocco. It's not them, I'll lay odds on it. I won't take any risks, but I'm going to bring them in nonetheless. We'll grill them both. Then when we get nothing from them and check their alibis, perhaps we can get back to doing some proper work."

"The address is Heron House, up on the tenth floor." Ruth took the slip of paper Calladine passed her. "There're the two boys and their mother."

"We'll keep an eye out first. I'd prefer not to cause too much of a stir. We'll bring them in, but quietly, and when we're done we'll return them in the same fashion. Ruth, take a wander around the community centre first, see who's doing what. Speak to the kids; see if you can find out where the Foxleys hang out. Try and find out if they've heard about Ice and Gavin yet, and if anyone's seen Mash."

Would anyone talk to her? Calladine and Rocco dropped Ruth off and watched as she disappeared through the centre's double doors.

* * *

The place was quiet — no groups meeting there today. She wandered through to the IT suite, which was quite busy. A group of teenagers were crowded around one machine, giggling. Looking at what? Surely they had porn filters, Ruth thought, as she approached them. A place like this —it was vital.

"Lads!" Immediately the screen they'd been watching went blank.

"Has anyone seen Mash?"

One of them managed a shrug, and the others studied their footwear.

"I wanted a word, that's all. Nothing heavy. He's due to have his tag off," she lied. "Thought I'd give him some advice, help him keep his nose clean from now on. You're Rob Storey aren't you?" She smiled at one lad. "I know your big brother and your dad."

"He's with Cuba somewhere, inne? Not seen 'em all day. Not been in 'ere."

The others nodded their agreement — so far so good.

"Dreadful business with Ice . . ."

Now they got really shifty, glancing sideways at one another, and then back to studying their feet.

"Gone — aren't they?" Rob ventured, keeping his eyes on the floor. "'eard they were both dead. Must of crossed someone big."

"Is that the word going round the estate?" she almost whispered.

He shrugged again. "Someone else running things now, but I can't say anything. Daren't, dare I?"

Won't say anything was more like it. But then who could blame them? They were young and frightened, things had changed and they needed to stay solid. What they didn't need was to be seen talking to the police. She should go.

"Okay, lads. If you do see Mash, tell him I want a word."

Even though Cuba had been found early that morning, they hadn't mentioned her. Hadn't word got out yet? That wasn't the way of a drugs war.

"Take care. Keep out of trouble." She walked away.

* * *

Calladine banged his fist repeatedly on the Foxleys' front door.

"Harassment, that," a woman yelled at them as she finally answered the knocking. "We've got nowt, we know nowt, so shove off! I don't want your sort bothering my boys."

"You've got this all wrong, Mrs Foxley. All we want is a little chat with your Liam and Josh. Not asking too much, is it?"

"Bugger off, they're not here."

"Are they hanging out somewhere on the estate perhaps?"

"How the fucking hell should I know? Now do one, or I'll shout the dog."

"I didn't think pets were allowed in these flats, Mrs Foxley," Rocco offered. "The houses, yes, but not the flats."

"We live here and we've got a dog. Anyone doesn't like it, let them come and tell me personally."

She was tall and thin and craned her neck forward, her face blazing red with anger as she issued the threat. Calladine shivered. God he'd hate to live here amongst this little lot. And the state of her — she had several front teeth missing and her sparse hair was already greying. What was she? Two teenage lads, had them young — somewhere in her mid-thirties? Some life, Calladine thought, groaning inwardly. They'd get nothing here.

"I still want to speak to them. I want to know what they've been doing over the last few weeks." He handed her his card. "Get one of them to ring me."

"Whatever it is you think they've done we weren't here, none of us were. We were in Spain, working. Don't believe me? Well check with the Border people. They'll tell you when we left and when we returned."

With that she retreated inside and slammed the door shut.

"Spain." Rocco mused. "Holiday, do you reckon? She didn't look as if she had two pennies to rub together, never mind the money that would take."

"Yes, Spain." Calladine sighed. She was probably telling the truth. He knew that Fallon had a villa in Andalucía; a huge rambling house up in the hills. What was the betting that they'd been working for him? But he'd check nonetheless.

"If it's not them, then who?" Rocco asked as they started down the stairs. "There is no one else — unless we put Mash in the frame. Perhaps that's why we can't find him. Perhaps he has done a runner."

"Mash wouldn't hurt Cuba. We can't find him because he's probably lying dead somewhere like the others. No doubt neatly filleted and frozen in a number of carrier bags by now. This isn't a drugs war, Rocco. Fallon has brought the Foxleys over to keep things running, but they aren't responsible for the murders."

Calladine phoned the incident room and instructed Imogen to get on to Border Control straight away. Jones needed to know that he was wrong. He needed to appreciate exactly what it was they were up against.

* * *

Malcolm Masheda's mother was at home. Ruth knocked on the front door and was let in moments later. The woman was beside herself with worry.

"Sergeant Ruth Bayliss, Leesworth Police." Ruth showed her warrant card. "I'm looking for Malcolm, Mrs Masheda. It's very important that I find him quickly."

"He's not here. He didn't come home all night." Mrs Masheda's voice was strained. "He's not a bad boy. He tries hard these days and doesn't come in late. I don't understand. No word, no message and his phone's dead. He has a tag — he's breached his conditions, so I'm really worried they'll lock him away this time."

"When exactly did you last see Malcolm?"

"Yesterday afternoon, about two it must have been, because I got the airport bus home. I've been visiting my sister in Trinidad — she's been ill. All the time I was gone he kept in touch. He texted so much his fingers must have hurt." She smiled. "But now I's home — nothing. It's not like him."

"We're looking for him too, Mrs Masheda. Something's happened . . . there's been an incident. Cuba Hassan was shot last night, in the alley beside this block."

"You think it was my Malcolm?" Her dark eyes were frantic. "That can't be right. He wouldn't do that. He loves Cuba. He knows I don't approve; her family is trash, but he still loves her."

"Yes I know he does. I'm going to arrange for an officer to keep an eye out — watch the block. If you hear from Malcolm, ring me straight away." Ruth handed over a card.

"If Cuba's been shot, then my Malcolm might be lying hurt somewhere. You must find him, Sergeant. You must bring him home to me."

Chapter 15

"Detective!" Lydia's seductive voice trilled in his ear. "I'm afraid I've got bad news."

"Go on, upset me." Given what she'd already been sent, bad probably meant *really* bad.

"I've received some photos this time — some rather nasty photos at that, and with some rather angry words to go with them. The angry words are directed at me, so I'm feeling somewhat edgy."

"Are you at the newspaper offices?"

"No, I'm waiting in your reception area at the station."

"I'll be with you shortly. Don't go anywhere; wait for me."

* * *

He met with Ruth and Rocco by the car park outside the community centre, and they swapped results.

"Mash didn't come home last night. His mother is desperate for us to find him," Ruth said.

"We've drawn a blank with the Foxleys too. I don't think they've anything to do with this and I don't think it'll take much work to prove it," Rocco reported.

"What now? We could check on Kelly again," Ruth asked.

"Okay, do that, but I've got to get back. Have another look around — see what forensics has turned up in that alley, see if they've got anything else. I'll send a car to pick you up. Our man has sent Lydia some more stuff — photos this time. I'll look at them and see you back at the station."

"Watch your step, sir. You do realise that you and the blonde are the nick's current hot topic?"

"I can't imagine why that would be, Sergeant — unless you've been blabbing." He narrowed his eyes in an effort to appear fierce.

"Me, sir? Soul of discretion, me. You know that." She nudged Rocco.

"I'm serious, Ruth," he said taking her to one side, out of Rocco's earshot. "Both you and me are skating on thin ice — you and the teacher and me with Lydia."

"Bring it on, that's what I say," she grinned. "Personally I'm quite enjoying myself and something tells me you are too."

"Just keep it quiet," he warned. "I don't want the team gossiping and stuff getting back to Jones, or worse."

Ruth tapped the side of her nose. "I'll dampen things down the moment I get back. It'll be a pleasure because it'll cheer Joyce up no end."

Pep talk over

Ruth and Rocco went into the community centre, chatting and laughing. So much for trying to keep your private life under wraps. Calladine shook his head.

Why Lydia? He didn't understand that one. How did the murderer know about her? She'd been there, yesterday, on the common. Had she been seen? Come to think about it, how had she known to go to the common in the first place? The crowd had only gathered because they'd seen the police tents. He'd not asked her, but perhaps he should do so before their relationship went any further.

"Show me." There was no time for small talk. "We've got a young man missing, so this could be important." She sighed, seeing his frown, and rearranged her belongings.

"I don't think you quite appreciate what I'm giving up for you, Detective. This story could make me."

He couldn't understand who would want such a thing. Who'd want to make a name for themselves on the back of such hideous brutality? He watched as she delved into a folder and pulled out the contents. What was her angle? So, she wanted the story, and he would try to help her. He'd put off holding a press briefing because he didn't want to cause panic on the estate, but this delay also gave her a head start. To date she was the only member of the press who had any clue as to what had happened.

"Another horrific montage, I'm afraid." She spread a number of photos along the bench she'd been sitting on, face up. "Your missing victim, perhaps?"

The photos were taken from various angles, showing what looked like human guts splattered on concrete flooring. Malcolm Masheda? He could only hope not.

"What did he write?" Calladine's voice was harsh, and he rubbed a hand over his weary head.

Lydia handed him a printed sheet. "There's not much, but what there is, it's to the point, don't you think?"

> *Why haven't you printed what I*
> *sent you, bitch! I won't warn you*
> *again.*

"This looks very much like a threat to me, Tom. I could be in danger. You will protect me, Detective?" She purred, cuddling up close to him. "Keep me under lock and key if you want, *your* lock and key, of course." She smiled, batting her long lashes at him.

"This is no joke, Lydia, so don't treat it as such. This man has murdered people in the most awful way. Look at this." He pointed to one of the photos. "Probably the latest victim — his guts all over the floor. I'll have to check with the doc but I expect he died slowly and painfully. Our man is a sadistic bastard, so imagine, just for a moment, the possibilities if he got hold of you."

"You're being a drama queen, Tom. How would he get hold of me? Go on tell me — because I'm rarely alone."

Bravado, he was sure of it, because she'd just delivered those words along with a meaningful shudder.

"You live in that apartment block alone. In fact most of those flats are still empty — too damned expensive."

"We have security — alarms, cameras — so I'm quite safe. Believe me, Tom, I take no risks."

"I'll have you watched. I'll put an officer outside your door."

"Perhaps I should just print it. Give him what he wants."

"Don't you dare! And don't even think of crossing me on this one. Do you understand, Lydia? I will feed the press what they need to know in small chunks and I certainly won't embellish what I tell them with images like this." He waved one of the photos in front of her face.

What was going on inside this bastard's head? Why did he want his crimes plastered across the front page?

"You hold everything until you get my say-so. But what I will do is hold a press briefing. Tell the lot of you a little of what's happened. Perhaps that'll hold him off for a while."

"Don't tell too much, please." She snuggled close again. "You know I want this. It's going to mark me out as the one to watch."

"If we're not careful you'll be marked out alright — marked out for murder. How did you know anyway? Yesterday morning? Who told you to go to the common?"

"I have my sources." She rolled her eyes. "And I'm not divulging them, because if I do I won't get anything else."

"I don't think you understand, Lydia. For reasons I can't work out yet, our man wants publicity, and he's trying to use you to get it. That's why he's sent you this stuff, and he chose well too. You're so damned hungry for a leg up that if I hadn't moderated your actions you would have printed this."

"You've no idea how all this works, Detective. I need people to talk to me — like you. I'm widely read. I have written several headline pieces lately, and I have a weekly column. People know me, Tom, and they know what I'm after. So they tell me things."

He wanted to ask her more, but his mobile rang.

"Sir?" Calladine greeted his boss, warily polite.

"Incident room, Tom. I want an update on your visit to the Hobfield. Now."

"I've got to go up. Get in your car and go straight back to your office. I'll arrange that briefing and ring you later. Don't leave work until we've spoken. This is no joke, Lydia." He gathered the photos together. "This guy, whoever he is, is one mean bastard and you don't want to be in his sights for next victim."

* * *

"So where are they, Tom?" Jones glared at him. "I said to bring them in and they're not in the cells."

"Not at home, and according to their mother all of them have just returned from Spain — been there for weeks working for Fallon. They'd be stupid to lie about something like that when it can be so easily checked out. So we're probably barking up the wrong tree."

"You've actually checked have you, before making that assumption?"

Jones wasn't impressed. His foot was tapping impatiently on the incident room floor.

"Imogen! How did you get on with Border Control?" Calladine called out to the DC, who was seated at her desk, head buried in some paperwork.

"Their systems are playing up, sir. They're going to ring me back."

Just what he needed. Now Jones would go in for the kill.

"Stop mucking about, Tom. Go and get them, and no excuses this time. I want those two in our cells within the next couple of hours, and I want Masheda found. Do I make myself clear?"

The red-faced DCI turned on his heel and strode back to his office He'd been one of them a few months ago, but now he wanted to impose his will on the station.

* * *

"Rocco, are you still on the estate?" Calladine asked.

"Yes, sir, we're in the community centre."

"Wait there. I'm coming back. Jones wants them brought in regardless."

Calladine thought Jones was a fool. He couldn't see what was staring him in the eye. Last year he'd have been fine with the theory that this wasn't a drugs war. He'd have helped — sent his own team to scout around. But a promotion had stifled what little detective instinct he'd had, and there was nothing left. Just as well he spent most of his time sitting behind that desk, because he sure as hell wasn't fit for anything else.

Calladine found Ruth and Rocco drinking coffee in the community centre café.

"Back to the Foxleys' flat." Their faces fell. "Jones's idea, not mine. Border Control are dragging their feet, so I've got nothing to throw at him but my instinct — and we all know what he thinks of that."

"No worries, sir." Rocco tossed his coffee down his throat. "We'll go back up and wait for the tearaways to return."

God knows when they'd be home. It was early evening and already dark. The tenth floor deck was deserted and cold. It acted like a wind tunnel for the icy blasts blowing all kinds of rubbish around in little whirlpools of debris. The boom of music, the sound of television programmes and a barking dog echoed around the bleak space. How long? Calladine wondered. And had Imogen got the information he needed yet? Pulling his mobile from his pocket, he texted her. No, she hadn't.

Ruth waited in the stairwell, her collar up against the harsh chill, clapping her gloved hands together for warmth. She looked pissed off. Voices carried round the corner — loud, male and heavy with expletives.

"I think they're coming."

The two youths passed her. She was huddled down in her coat, and they didn't give her a second look. Once they'd passed, she gave Calladine the thumbs up.

"Liam Foxley, Josh Foxley," Calladine walked forward to greet them. "Detective Inspector Calladine, Leesworth Police. This is DC Rockliffe. Can we have a word? Won't keep you long. Just a little help with some enquiries we're making."

"Get lost." Liam Foxley spat onto the deck. "Don't talk to coppers, so do one."

"It's in your own interests to talk to us this time, son." Calladine was trying hard not to get riled.

"He said get lost, so go on, fuck off!" Their mother suddenly appeared in the doorway. She stood, framed against the pool of light from inside, hanging onto the leash of a huge dog. It was trying hard to pull her out, almost winning the battle.

"Go on. Leave us alone or I'll let the dog off."

"Mrs Foxley, I don't think you understand. As it is I just want to clear one or two things up, but if you persist with this attitude then things will get a lot heavier."

"Too bloody right they will." She stepped out onto the deck, allowing the beast of a dog to lunge forward. "Now get lost or I'll do for you."

"Don't threaten me, Mrs Foxley."

"I've had enough, heard enough and got better things to do. Sling your hook!" She produced a vodka bottle from behind her back. "Go on — fuck off, the bloody lot of you!"

Rocco made to move forward — whether to warn her again, or remonstrate with her, Calladine had no idea, but in one swift movement she struck him across the side of the head. He fell heavily to the ground. Josh Foxley let out a yell and kicked Rocco viciously in the stomach as he leapt past him to follow his mother and brother inside.

Calladine was on his mobile instantly, as Ruth rushed forward to kneel beside Rocco.

"Backup and ambulance needed, floor ten, Heron House, officer down!" Then he crouched beside his stricken colleague.

"Rocco?" Ruth whispered, dabbing his bleeding head with a tissue. "Can you hear me? Help's coming. We'll get you to hospital. It won't be long. Hang in there, Rocco."

Ruth looked into Calladine's face with eyes that were full of tears. Rocco hadn't deserved this. He wasn't moving; he was out cold, and the lurching in his stomach told him it was bad. The inspector slipped off his overcoat and placed it over the DC.

* * *

Ruth went to the hospital with Rocco, sitting beside him holding his hand all the way. Calladine took his car and went back to the station. There was nothing left to do on the Hobfield. Backup had arrived, battered down the Foxleys' front door and carted the three of them off in handcuffs.

The thing was, he knew it could all have been avoided. If Jones had listened — listened to reason —

instead of wanting him to dive head first into that bear pit, then Rocco wouldn't have been injured.

"Border Control got back," Imogen told him as she fastened up her coat in preparation to leave for the day. "You were right. They've all been in Spain the last six months."

Calladine grabbed the short printout, along with the newspaper page from Lydia, and marched into Jones's office.

"This is a bloody mess. Do you realise DC Rockliffe has been carted off unconscious because of our run in with that damn family? When are you going to start listening to reason, Jones? I told you it wasn't them from the off."

"Watch your tongue, Detective Inspector. Regrettable, but I had no way of knowing how volatile that family was."

"Regrettable. Is that all you've got to say? It's a bloody farce, that's what it is. I told you they've been working for Fallon. They've been in Spain like they said."

Calladine thrust the printout into the DCI's face and then dealt out the photos from Lydia as if they were a pack of cards.

"What do I have to produce to convince you? The Foxleys weren't even in the country. It wasn't them, alright? The photos — highly likely that's Malcolm Masheda — see, same MO, guts all over the place. They were sent to Lydia Holden within the last few hours."

He stood back, shaking with anger and pent up frustration. The man was a damned fool!

"She needs watching too. She's been threatened. I want an officer outside her door."

"That can't happen I'm afraid. We haven't the manpower and even if we had, there's the cost implication."

"What? How do you put a cost on a young woman's life? We're dealing with a brutal killer. I don't know what's at the back of all this, but Lydia Holden has been picked out as his mouthpiece for the publicity he wants. She hasn't delivered, so she's in danger. What do you want, sir? Another mutilated dead body — or this?" He shook the front page mock-up.

Jones's face went ashen. "That can't go out," he mumbled and coughed his throat clear.

"Well that's what he wants, and Lydia Holden is supposed to print it."

"Call a press conference for tomorrow morning. We'll give them something, but not that." Jones's eyes were glazed as he stared at the details. "I'd better have a look at the case notes and review what you've got so far."

"What we've got is nothing, but the one thing I am sure of is that this isn't to do with gangs or drugs. The victims are being picked off for a reason. I've still got enquiries to make, and Doc Hoyle hasn't finished with the bodies yet, so we have to stay hopeful. But whoever is doing this is clever, sir. I don't think it's random. Something links these three. I just have to find out what that something is."

Chapter 16

"I've got those names, sir." Dodgy placed a printed list on Calladine's desk.

He'd wanted to leave early to check on Lydia; make sure she was okay, given that the police could offer no proper protection. However, both the day and the night were disappearing fast. Now he'd have to check through the list and follow up any possible leads it might give. They were running out of time.

"Thanks." He nodded to the young officer, already scanning down the column of names.

"I think I'm going mad!" he exclaimed, holding his head in his hands. "My own mother's on this list." What was going on? Calladine picked up the phone and dialled Monika's number.

"You never told me my mother's on Aricept. I'm looking at a list, and she's the only one in the home taking the drug. Why's that?"

"And *hi* to you too, Tom. She's on it because your mother is a good candidate for the drug. It's not for every case of Alzheimer's. She's still in the early stages, you see, and it's hoped that the Aricept will hold it at bay for a while and improve her quality of life in the long term."

Long term? She is eighty-five for heaven's sake!

"But shouldn't you have told me?"

"Why? You've never shown an interest in what she takes before. From time to time she's on a number of different drugs — painkillers, antibiotics — you know the type of thing. I rarely tell you about any of those."

"Does she take Risedronate?"

"No, she doesn't, but it is dispensed to some of our other residents. Unlike the Aricept it's a commonly prescribed drug. Is all this important, Tom? I can give you a report on what she's had over the last twelve months if you like."

"Sorry, Monika, that's not necessary. This isn't really about my mum — it's the case I'm working on. The bodies were full of drugs and one of them was Aricept."

"That should narrow it down considerably for you, then. We have only the one user here, and you can cross your mum off the list of suspects. She can barely walk — remember?"

"Very droll. I don't think a user of Aricept did this. I think their drugs were stolen by someone close to them."

"In that case talk to their GPs. If a patient isn't taking the drug properly, then they'll know. Aricept is usually prescribed by a hospital doctor, so there will be check-ups and they'd notice it wasn't having the desired effect."

That wasn't a bad idea.

"Sorry, Monika. I'm not getting at you. I've had a pig of a day. One of my team has been injured. Poor Rocco is in hospital with a head injury. Look — shall I come over tonight? We can have a catch up and flop in front of the telly."

"Sounds nice. I don't see nearly enough of you these days, Tom. Come when you're ready. I'll make something good and hot."

Calladine left his office and went to find Dodgy. "Contact these people's GPs and find out if any of them are not responding properly to the drug Aricept. Leave it to the morning if you like and put your findings on my desk. I'm nipping out for a bit."

Before he called it a day he needed to check on Lydia. She'd be finishing work soon and making for her apartment. He couldn't spend another night with her, but at least he could make sure she was locked up tight.

"Sir!" Imogen called out, the office phone in her hand. "Ruth wants you — says it's urgent."

"Tom, Rocco's in a bad way." She was crying. "He's been taken to theatre and his parents are here. It looks bad. They know because he's blown a pupil or something. I don't know what to say to them. They're so upset."

"I'll come. Give me ten minutes or so and I'll be there."

He handed the phone back to Imogen and went to get his coat. If Rocco couldn't be fixed he'd never forgive himself. He should have told Jones where to go, stood his ground. He should never have gone back to bring the Foxleys in.

"Tell Jones, one of you. I won't be back until the morning. Don't forget — if Kelly turns up, then let me know at once."

* * *

Ruth was pacing the corridor outside the operating theatre with Greg and Jean Rockliffe, Rocco's parents.

"What've they said?"

"He's had a significant bleed; something called a subdural hematoma, and a blood clot has formed. They need to remove it straight away, then it's a waiting game. He'll be in intensive care for a while, and then we'll have to see."

"Thanks Ruth." Calladine turned to the parents. "Look, Mr and Mrs Rockliffe, Rocco — Simon — was unlucky. He wasn't being stupid or taking any chances, none of us could have known what was going to happen.

He was simply there — stood in the wrong place when that mad woman lashed out."

Jean Rockliffe put her hand on his arm. "We know that Simon's job is risky, Inspector, and he's told us often enough how you take care of them all. It's not your fault. You can't blame yourself for every mishap that befalls your team."

Some bloody mishap! What had Ruth said — subdural hematoma? He'd no idea how long it'd be before Rocco was back on his feet, but it sure as hell wouldn't be any time soon.

"Can I get anyone a drink while we wait?"

"No need for you to hang around, Inspector." Jean Rockliffe smiled. "I know it's serious, but my boy's strong. He'll be fine."

He could tell from her face that she wasn't convinced. With an injury like that, who would be?

"I'll get some teas." He didn't know what to say to her. The truth was, despite her kind words, he did blame himself. He'd allowed Jones to call the shots, even though he knew it was wrong. Not a mistake he'd make again.

He couldn't face them. He couldn't walk back, proffer tea and make small talk. He passed by the tea machine in the corridor and went to find Doc Hoyle in the mortuary.

"Sebastian!" He greeted the man with a weak smile. "Sorry to burst in on you like this. I didn't know where to go. I've had a bad day — no, much worse than that — a crap day, the very worst. One of my own is in theatre with a brain injury."

The pathologist shook his head and gestured to a chair.

"Sit down. I'll get you a drink. What have they said? Which of your team is it?"

"Rocco. A damned good cop, too. I just can't call this . . . I don't know how it will pan out. Brain injuries are difficult to predict."

"They'll have got in a Neuro team from Oldston. They're some of the best, Tom. If he can be put right then they're the ones to do it. Believe me, I've seen some wonderful stuff achieved."

"We really need this one to break. It's doing my head in to be honest. And now this happens. His parents are waiting outside theatre with Ruth. I should be with them, but his mum is being so damned reasonable I just had get away. Despite what she says, it was my fault. I should have stopped it. I should have known what would happen. It was like walking into a cage of wild animals."

Hoyle measured out some whiskey into a glass.

"Hindsight is there only to taunt us, Tom. We do what we can. You have a situation, and you react as you see fit. Here, get this down you. The lad will be okay. Most are, you know."

Calladine threw the amber fluid down his throat in one. It burned a comforting path down to his stomach. He held the glass out for more.

"Sorry. This isn't the usual me. Frankly, tonight I just want to get hammered and forget the whole hellish business."

"Damned expensive malt, this is, Tom." The doctor's dark eyes twinkled as he measured out some more. "And we can't have you drunk on duty, can we?"

"Right now, Doc, I don't care. I just want Rocco to recover and for us to find the bastard who's ripping his way through the estate, and then get a good night's sleep."

"It's not going to be easy. Whoever is doing this is meticulous. He's left no biological trace whatsoever."

"So he is forensically aware?"

"Very much so. In fact I'd go so far as to say his crimes are perpetrated in a forensic suit, hat, and gloves — the lot. When he takes them he won't be able to be so careful; he obviously can't draw attention to himself. But given that we've never found any of the victim's clothing, he probably burns it. The hair — what's left on the head

— and the body parts are clean too. It's as if they'd been washed or hosed down before freezing."

"I take it the parts we've got are Edwards and Hurst?"

"Certainly Edwards, but we have no DNA on record for Hurst. But we do have two bodies only, and, given they were rarely apart, it's fairly safe to assume that the other is Hurst."

"Thanks. Can I have your report fairly quick? Keep Jones happy. Not that he bloody well deserves it after today."

"I'll email it to you tomorrow, Inspector. Now — do you want more whiskey or are you able to rejoin the others?"

Truth was, Calladine felt a little woozy. The drink had gone straight to his head — which wasn't surprising because he hadn't eaten all day. He checked his watch: gone nine. Monika would be wondering where he'd got to.

"I'll get them some tea and go back. Talk tomorrow, Doc. And thanks." On the way back he rang Monika and told her what had happened. She still wanted to see him.

"Come anyway. It doesn't matter what time you roll in. You can stay, you know. You have slept with me before, and anyway I want to discuss your mum. She's been a bit upset today; a friend of hers has died, and she could do with seeing her son pretty soon."

So that was the deal. He'd finish up here and then go round to Monika's. He got the tea, plus a coffee for himself, and went to see how things were going.

"Apparently they've nearly finished, and it's looking okay. He won't be able to talk to us for a while; they're going to keep him sedated. So we might as well go." Ruth was smiling with relief.

His own relief flowed through him with almost as much warmth as the whiskey — and with much the same effect. He was feeling distinctly spaced out. Calladine said goodbye to Rocco's parents and walked back to the car park with Ruth.

"I'm going to Monika's."

"Hope you don't intend to drive yourself. I can smell you from here. Who's been feeding you the booze, you lucky bugger?"

"Doc Hoyle keeps a stash in his filing cabinet. Can you believe that — a pathologist with a penchant for illicitly stashed liquor?"

"Shame I didn't come with you. I've got a damn cold coming and a wee dram would do me good. Anyway, I'd better give you a lift. Go have a word with the security guy over there about leaving your car here, and I'll go and get mine.'

It didn't take long to get to Monika's, but by the time they arrived Calladine was nearly asleep. Ruth tooted her horn and she came out to get him.

"Silly sod's been downing the whiskey. You might have to put him straight to bed."

Chapter 17

Thursday

They sat on stage in a row behind a long desk. DCI George Jones was in the middle. Calladine hadn't expected so much interest, but there they were — hordes of press people, all curious and baying for information.

The noise was growing — and his pain increased as it passed through his throbbing head. Two whiskeys and a few beers at Monika's had left him with a hangover. He kept looking around, at the seats, at the reporters still piling in through the door, but there was no sign of Lydia.

She wouldn't miss this — and he'd made sure she'd been told. So where was she? It was a few minutes to ten; just time to ring her. He tried her mobile first. It was turned off. He dialled her home number and after an endless wait, a female voice answered.

"Lydia?"

"No — this is Katya. Miss Holden has left for her office."

"And you are?"

"Katya."

Had she understood? Her accent was Eastern European, possibly Polish. "When was that?" "She left early. She has a busy day. Will you leave a message?"

"No thanks. I'll catch her at her office."

He dialled again. "Lydia Holden, please."

"She's not here yet."

"Is she coming straight to the press briefing at the police station?"

"Not sure. We've sent Morton. I think Miss Holden must be running late this morning."

But she wasn't. According to Katya she'd left early. What was going on? Where was she?

He pushed his folder of notes under Jones's nose and nudged him.

"I'm going to have to leave, sir. I can't find Lydia Holden so I'm going to check her apartment."

"You can't leave now, Tom. What on earth's got into to you? They'll have questions, and what the hell do I tell them?"

There was an answer to that, but Calladine swallowed it.

"Ruth's here." He nodded at her. "Anything tricky, get her to deal with it."

He wasn't prepared to argue or to waste any more time. He got up from the table, grabbed his coat and left.

* * *

It took no more than fifteen minutes to drive through Leesdon, along the bypass and into Hopecross village. He left his car parked at the side of the road and pressed the buzzer to gain access to the building.

"Katya! Police! Let me in."

Katya, it turned out, was employed to do a little cleaning and shopping for Lydia. She came in three days a week.

"You spoke to her this morning?"

"Yes, I made toast while she dressed. We spoke about what she'd make for dinner, and then she left."

"What time?"

"Before eight. I arrive at about seven thirty."

"Did she take her car?"

"Yes, she took her keys. See they are gone."

"Where does she leave her car?"

"In the car park, at the back of the building. Each apartment has a designated parking space. Miss Holden's is 44."

"Okay. Thanks Katya. Here's my card. If you think of anything else that's relevant, then ring me."

Calladine hurtled down the staircase and out through the back doors. It was a sizeable parking area, but there was only one car left in it — Lydia's.

He felt his stomach seize. He strode forward, snapping on a pair of latex gloves. Was this a crime scene? He prayed not. He hoped that the sick feeling in his stomach and the thoughts swirling in his head were entirely misplaced.

The car was still locked, and the engine stone cold. It hadn't moved. His instincts were right; something had happened to Lydia. He called the incident room.

"Imogen. Lydia Holden's gone missing. I want a full forensic team at Wrigley Mill Apartments car park, and will you tell Ruth to join me the minute the press briefing is finished."

Calladine went back inside. Lydia had said there were alarms and cameras. So where were they? And how soon could he get his hands on the footage?

It didn't take long. Within the hour forensics were crawling all over the place. Calladine and a snuffly Ruth sat in front of a screen in the caretaker's office, preparing to watch the video from the last few hours.

"Thanks for dropping me in it, sir." She sneezed and sat down heavily beside him. "Those press people. They practically had me for breakfast, vicious lot of harpies that they are. And I wasn't at my best. I've got this bug and I feel dreadful . . . not that anyone cares. And do you know how stupid that man Jones is? DCI or not, he's still got a lot to learn. They asked if he — the man we're looking for — is considered still active and dangerous, and he tells them — yes! I mean, no effort made to stop the panic. No not him. By the time he'd finished he might as well have given them that bloody bimbo's front page."

"That *bloody bimbo* has gone missing, remember?" He was angry — not with Ruth, but with the way things were going. He should be able to sort this out — so why couldn't he? Why was this so difficult? The doc had agreed that their man was forensically aware. Did that imply, perhaps, that he had a degree of training? Perhaps he'd worked in a lab, a hospital — or even for the police . . .

"There." Ruth pointed to the screen. "She's just left through the back entrance doors."

They both watched the young woman walk towards her car. She wore a dark fitted suit with a short skirt and high heels. She looked lovely, her blonde hair swished on her shoulders. She carried a briefcase in one hand and had her bag over her shoulder.

Suddenly there was someone else. At first, nothing more than a shadow cast across the tarmac in the weak morning sunshine. Then a man stepped into view. He was wearing jeans and a casual jogging top with the hood up and pulled well down over his face at the front. He had his hands in his pockets and walked steadily behind Lydia.

Calladine's heart was in his mouth. He didn't want to see her hurt. If the bastard hit her he didn't know what his reaction would be.

But he didn't. It was almost as if he'd simply whispered something in her ear. He crept very close, leaned forward and spoke a few words. She turned. The camera caught her full in the face as she smiled, chatting happily to the stranger. Perhaps he wasn't a stranger. She laughed — she actually laughed; then opened the boot of her car and put her briefcase in it.

He kept his back to the camera. The bastard knew damn well it was there and that the footage would be scrutinised later. He took her arm. She was still smiling as she happily walked off with him.

She was gone and they had nothing. He could get the images blown up so that they filled the entire wall, but all he had was a rear view of the man. He was clever. When, if ever, was he going to slip up? But then something occurred to him. Lydia had been facing the camera. If they could get someone in who could lip-read, then perhaps they could decipher what she'd said to him. It might give them something. Good idea — he'd get Imogen on it straight away.

* * *

"I think you should take her today, Tom. She's been very upset since she heard about Lizzie, and the funeral is bound to make her more so."

He'd only just got back to his desk when Monika rang him.

"Lizzie Mottram, I remember her. She was a neighbour. I used to call her auntie and she'd give us — me and you know who — sweets. Ma liked Lizzie. So when is it?"

"Twelve noon, at the crematorium. We'll wrap her up warm and one of the carers will accompany you both. Your mum will be in a wheelchair, so you shouldn't have any bother getting her about."

Today. It would be, wouldn't it? Just when he was up to his ears in it.

"What about afterwards?"

"Back to Lizzie's son's for a bite to eat. But don't drink anything. You had quite enough last night, remember?"

146

Well no, he didn't remember. Last night was all a bit of a blur. The shock of Rocco, the spat with Jones and working all hours — it'd taken its toll, and the drink had affected him badly. He'd had a raging head all morning. It was only the shock of Lydia's disappearance and the urgent need to find her that was keeping him going.

"You do realise that I don't really have the time. I've got a missing reporter. So I might have to give the wake a miss."

"Do what you can and perhaps we can try again tonight? I would like to wake up next to you tomorrow — you know — it being my birthday."

Bugger! He'd completely forgotten. That meant, as well as everything else, he'd have to tear along to the Antiques Centre, as Ruth had suggested earlier in the week.

Dodgy stuck his head around the office door. "No luck with the GPs, sir. All those patients are doing just fine and improving on the drug." He snuffled, taking a hankie from his pocket.

"You got it too, lad? Don't you dare go taking time off. I don't care if you're dead on your feet. With Rocco laid up, I want the rest of you focused on this."

Dodgy nodded, screwing up his face to hold back a sneeze.

Calladine went to find Brad Long.

"I need your help. I want some bodies to collect the CCTV from the High Street in Hopecross. I want the cars clocking. I want special attention paid to those with two occupants — a man and a woman. This woman." He handed across a photo of Lydia. "She's blonde, a stunner, so she's hard to miss. They may have used a car, or they might even have been on foot. Either way, will you get your people to check it out?"

"This is the babe who came here looking for you." Long smirked. "Done a runner has she? Got wind of what you're really like, Inspector, and had it away on her toes?"

"No, idiot. She's been taken by the bastard who did this." He held out the front page mock up. "So less of the backchat, please, and try to be of some help."

Calladine watched Long's expression change as he scanned the sheet. He could only hope the silly bugger would see the urgency of this and be of some real help.

"See what you mean. Up against it this time — must be stretching even your powers of deduction." He sighed and slammed the mock newssheet under the photocopier lid and pressed the switch. "Consider it done, old mate." He handed Calladine the original. "I'll get them right on it. Anything we get will be on your desk, pronto."

"Just ring me. He's a dangerous sod, and we're running out of time."

Chapter 18

"I never liked that one." Freda Calladine watched as another elderly lady was wheeled past them. "Look at her. Out of it on some drug or other. Bloody dementia, gets us all in the end. She's as hopeless as her daughter was; bloody hopeless the whole family. In the end the daughter paid the price, but she was no help to that grandson of hers."

"Who, Ma? Who are you talking about?"

"Her. Annie something or other. Knew her years ago. She had a weary, pathetic sort of a daughter. She had to go away after the son died. Wish I could remember her name . . . Annie . . . Annie . . . No, it won't come."

Calladine had no idea what she was on about. His head still hurt so he simply made sympathetic noises in response to his mother's ramblings.

"Morpeth, Brenda Morpeth — that was her married name. Can't remember what her other name was, her maiden name." She poked a withered finger at a woman who was being bundled into a car. "Her daughter, the Morpeth woman, killed herself in the end."

Calladine's eyes shot open. He stopped pushing and knelt down in front of his mother. "Did you say Morpeth, Ma?"

She nodded and pulled the woollen blanket further up her body. "Cold. Bloody freezing it is. Mind you, it always is in these places."

"Tell me about her, Ma. Does she live around here?"

"No, she's dead, I told you. She's dead and the boy's dead too — a long time ago. Annie never got over it, I expect. I wouldn't have either, but at least she's got the other one."

"Other one? What do you mean?"

"The other boy. Are you thick or summat today, son? You need to sharpen your wits — wake up a bit and listen."

She wasn't wrong on that one. So there'd been two Morpeth boys. Perhaps Ruth had been right to investigate that particular thread. He'd check him out once he got back to the station and see what Ruth had come up with. He wanted to know what had become of him, and he could also do with knowing that elderly woman's full name.

"Did she find you?"

"Who, Ma?"

"That young woman — your daughter, I think she said she was."

Calladine smiled and patted her shoulder. "I don't have a daughter, Ma, remember?"

"Sorry, son, I forgot. But she was asking about you."

Calladine left his mother with the carer. She'd take her to the wake and then back to the home. He drove to the station, feeling like death. Perhaps he was coming down with this damn virus too. Everyone else was.

* * *

"Ruth. The Morpeth boy — what have you got?"

"Not much. Only what we know from the original report. Nothing wrong with the investigation either. Everything was done correctly — just nothing to incriminate Edwards or Hurst."

"Imogen! Would you look through the records — you know, births and the like. I want to know what David Morpeth's grandmother's full name is. I know she's still alive. She was at the funeral I attended today. I also want to know where she lives and who takes care of her."

"Right, sir. I'll get straight on it."

It would mean Imogen searching through the records and then the electoral roll to find the address.

"I've got someone coming in later — about the lip-reading. A Mrs Hampshire, from the National Society for the Deaf."

"Good. Give me a shout when she gets here."

He had no idea where to even start looking for Lydia and was finding it difficult to cope with. If she got hurt — or worse — he'd never be able to forgive himself. He felt responsible. He should have done something about the press coverage — given the killer what he wanted. He should also have made Jones appoint an officer to watch her. Instead, he'd done nothing and now she'd disappeared.

He looked through the case file and studied the incident board again. Names. Faces. What was it he was missing? The answer to that one was simple enough: motive. Why was this bastard doing this? What had got to him so much that he'd felt the need to butcher those youths in such a dreadful way?

Imogen approached him. "Nothing. I know that's not what you want to hear, but believe me I've been through everything. There is no record for a woman marrying a man with the surname Morpeth within the last hundred years."

Calladine groaned. Every damned path led to a dead end.

"Are you absolutely sure? Could you have missed it?"

"No, sir. The records are all computerised. It's an easy enough process, and I've been on to all the register offices within a twenty mile radius. There is nothing — nothing at all. It is possible that she married abroad — or didn't marry at all."

No use checking the electoral roll then. No use whatsoever.

"I'll go and have another word with my mum. See if her mind has cleared any."

Ruth looked up at them from a file of notes. "I started this Morpeth thing. Perhaps I should come with you?"

"Not with that cold, you don't. You'll have them all at death's door within the week. You stay here. Look at those old case notes again and see if there's anything else we can use."

"You think this is significant, don't you, sir?"

"Truth is, I don't know what I think anymore. We've got nothing, so it's grab what we can time."

Fair enough. She'd do what she could.

* * *

It was teatime at the home when he arrived. His mum was back from the funeral and settled in her chair in the lounge.

"Tom!" She greeted him with a big smile. "I've been out — Lizzie Mottram's funeral, and then we had sherry at her son's house. Nice it is too, up on the hill, lovely view."

"Yes, Ma, I know where you've been. I was there, remember?"

Freda Calladine shook her head and sipped at her tea.

"We saw that other woman — the one with the pathetic daughter. Do you remember that?" he asked. "Do you remember her name, Ma?" It was a slim chance but it did no harm asking.

She gave him a quizzical look and offered him a biscuit. "Were you there, Tom? I don't remember seeing you. You should have said something."

Calladine closed his eyes, in a silent prayer for help. This was farcical. He couldn't go on like this.

"And she's been here again, your daughter."

"Not mine, Ma." He gently patted her knee. "I'll see you later."

More nothing. Surely this case had to break sometime. By the law of averages, one of the leads he followed up must eventually give him something.

* * *

"Mrs Hampshire's arrived. We set up in here so we can use the big screen," Imogen told him when he arrived back in the incident room.

The lip-reader, Clare Hampshire, was what Calladine would describe as a *comfortable* woman; a bit like Monika. She was middle-aged, slightly overweight, with short easy-to-manage hair, which she spiked a little on the top. Her nod to fashion, he reckoned. She wore no makeup apart from some pale pink lipstick, which gave her a washed out look.

They shook hands and sat down. Calladine explained what they were after: basically anything she could give them.

"She's a very animated young woman," Clare Hampshire began. "She's surprised to see him, but not shocked or frightened, I'd say."

"So she knows him?"

"Possibly. Either that, or he was expected. She's just said the word *detective*, followed by . . . *my overprotective detective*."

She obviously meant him. Lydia must have thought he'd sent the guy to look after her. She was so trusting. He wished she'd phoned him, made sure.

The lip-reader interpreted Lydia's speech:

Where are we going? — okay then, surprise me. But perhaps you can't say — safe house is it?

This was awful. Having to sit and watch as Lydia was so completely taken in. This man was good. There was no denying that. He was obviously pretending to be a

153

policeman. He was pulling it off with consummate ease and utter confidence.

"What was that?" Calladine leapt to his feet. "What was that sort of shudder as he leant forward?"

"It could be anything, sir. The camera was jolted — by the wind or something." Ruth sneezed into a tissue.

"That's it! The bastard sneezed. He bloody well sneezed, and she's still got hold of her briefcase, see it's in her hand!"

Calladine was jubilant. This was possibly the long-awaited breakthrough. He ran and picked up the office phone to call the forensic scientist.

"Julian! We've got him. He sneezed close to Lydia's briefcase. There must be drops of saliva and God knows what all over it. It's in the boot of her car. Our people are still there, so go get it."

Finally they'd had a stroke of luck — luck they so badly needed. Now they'd get his DNA. If their good fortune stuck then there might be a match on the database. He'd keep his fingers crossed, along with everything else.

Chapter 19

This wasn't right. Something was definitely wrong. Her mind was in a muddle. Where had she been? Where should she be now? There'd been a man; Tom had sent him. He was going to take her somewhere, but he hadn't done what he'd said he would. That was it. He was supposed to look after her, take her to the police station or somewhere safe. So what had changed? What had gone wrong?

Lydia Holden felt cold and heavy. She couldn't move her legs or her arms, and it was dark. The first wave of sheer panic rushed through her. What if? No. That was too dreadful to even contemplate.

"Anyone there?" she called into the cold space. "Where are you? I know someone's there. Please let me go."

He hadn't gagged her. He didn't want to obstruct her lovely face; he liked looking at her. He liked the sound of her soft, lilting voice.

"You're okay. No need to worry, Lydia. For now, that is." He leaned in close to her and chuckled.

She could feel his breath on her cheek. Smell him. But she couldn't see. Lydia felt the goosebumps form: fear. Who was he and what did he want? Then she remembered.

He'd come to her apartment; met her in the car park. She knew him, but couldn't think where from.

"Sorry to interrupt your day, Miss Holden. You must understand how it is. It's not my fault that you're here, that I've had to abduct you like this. The fault is entirely yours — well yours and that meddling inspector you're so fond of."

"I'm sorry. If I've done something to upset you, then I apologise."

She heard him laugh again and the sound of boots striding across a solid floor.

"You should try that again, this time with some real feeling behind it. You see, I wish you could convince me. I do so want to believe you, sweeting, I really do . . ." Sweeting was a term of endearment he usually reserved for his mother. He brushed his hand across her cheeks. "But you're lying, I know you are. Your type always does. All you really want is a story. And now — in the predicament you're in — you're simply trying to save your precious skin, aren't you?"

Lydia sobbed. She'd pushed things too far. He must have watched her — her and Tom — so he'd know that the inspector would never allow her to print the stuff he'd sent. This maniac wanted his brutality broadcast loud and long, and she'd dug her heels in. That's why she was here.

"And what beautiful skin you've got, too. So smooth. So perfect. And what magnificent breasts." His grip was hard, and it elicited a piercing scream from Lydia.

She was lying flat on her back — naked — on some sort of table; that's why she was so cold. He must have undressed her while she was unconscious. She struggled, trying to free one of her hands, but couldn't. So she wasn't only naked, but bound tight and spread-eagled. She became aware of this with a mix of horror and embarrassment.

"Now, now, sweeting, don't fuss so. You like men touching you, I know you do. You liked it when that meddling inspector touched you. It'll be no different with me. Just a little more — adventurous — that's all."

What did he mean by that? By now she was terrified. The goosebumps were at it again and that sick feeling in her stomach. She knew well enough what he meant; he was a man wasn't he?

"Don't hurt me," she begged. "Please, I'll do anything — print anything you want me to, but don't hurt me."

Lydia felt his hot breath on her cheeks as he laughed in her face. She was at his mercy. All she had to fight him with were words, and they were useless because he was clever, he'd know that she didn't mean any of them. He had the upper hand and he knew it. He'd think her a stupid bitch for falling for the lies he'd spun her.

"We should have some fun, you and I," he said softly. "I'd like that, wouldn't you, Lydia?"

She felt his hands travel the length of her body. They lingered on her breasts. Lydia tried to shrink down into the bench, his touch was sickening.

"I like your breasts, they're large but naturally so. I like your nipples too, hard rosy nipples that'll be good to taste."

Lydia screamed as he lowered his head, took one between his teeth and pulled lightly. "Get off me, you filthy bastard," she shrieked.

"How the lady roars," he laughed. "But soon, Lydia, I'll give you real reasons to scream. You will scream long and hard but no one will hear."

"Please — don't do this. Let me go, let me help you."

At that he laughed out loud. "No — why should I? I have you safe, in a secret place where no one will find you. Don't you find that as big a turn on as I do, Lydia?"

No she didn't, but the madman was not for listening. Lydia racked her brain for something she could say that would appeal to his better nature — if he had one. She'd seen the pictures, watched the film, she knew what he'd done to his other victims.

"It'll be good. You'll enjoy our time together. I know I shall. A female body is so much more interesting than a male one, don't you think? It offers up such fascinating possibilities when it comes to causing pain."

"You don't have to hurt me. We can be friends, we really can. I'll try hard, harder than before. I can be the woman you want; I can write your story and then everyone will understand. You can talk to me, I will be your mouthpiece."

Her voice was shaky, full of fear. She barely sounded convincing to herself, never mind to him. She screwed her eyes tightly shut, as if trying to turn him off, but it was no good. He was touching her again. The trembling started and became visible shaking as his hands continued their steady exploration of her body. "Stop this. Stop it now and I'll give you what you want." But her voice had become a high-pitched wail that simply made him laugh all the more.

Lydia knew this was hopeless. He wasn't going to stop. He wasn't going to stop until he'd taken everything — her body, her sanity . . . and then he'd do to her what he'd done to the others. She sobbed into the darkness and swore at him, her fists clenched in anger but totally useless.

"And what do you think I want, Lydia? Because I'm not entirely sure I know myself, anymore."

"You want your side of things printed in my paper. I can do that for you," she promised frantically. "I can make people see, make them know who you are." She was trying to sound as persuasive as she could.

He laughed again, the sound echoing against the bare stone walls. "And what do you think people will see? How will you make them understand? I've killed people, Lydia. I've butchered them in the most hideous ways. Turn your head — go on, just a little. Hanging on the wall just a few feet away is what's left of Mr Masheda. That's his bowels lying festering on the floor. So you see, sweeting, people won't like that; they won't like that at all. They'll want to lock me up and throw away the key."

Lydia squinted into the gloom. She could just make out the shape, the shape of a body, hanging like a rag doll from a hook. Seeing it, knowing what it was, instantly made her aware of the smell. She retched.

"I might still be able to sort it out." Who was she kidding? "We could try. I'll get some help, someone to come over and we can talk this through."

He didn't reply

His hands wandered lower down her body, and she screamed.

"I'll make you scream, alright. I'll make you wish you'd never been born. You should have printed what I sent you. If you'd done what you were supposed to, you wouldn't be here."

He ripped off his latex gloves and threw them to the floor. It was as though he wanted to feel her skin against his fingertips.

"We must send your inspector a little memento . . ." He palmed her breasts, now with his bare hands. Yes, that was better. "He'll be missing you. Perhaps one of your nipples? An apt little reminder of your time together. What do you think?"

Lydia whimpered and struggled against the restraints. He was mad. She'd been taken by the same madman who'd killed the others. This was hopeless. His hands were crawling all over her, and she felt sick. They were on her belly, then on her legs, between her thighs.

"No, on second thoughts, I like them too much. They're going to give me a lot of pleasure. Not a nipple. I'll think of something else."

She shrieked into the dark and begged him to stop but he didn't. He couldn't, not now. This was just too good. He put his face to within a few centimetres of hers and mouthed the words *stupid bitch*.

"You can't stop me, no one can. And now for the best bit — I'm going to have you."

"Nooooo!" Lydia screamed into the darkness. "Please no — not like this. You can't want this, not really."

She could hear his breathing and the fast beat of her own heart but there was something else — a buzzing noise, loud and insistent. He was being called away by someone. She heard him curse and felt a sharp slap across her thigh.

"I'll be back after I've sorted her out."

Chapter 20

"Anything yet?" Calladine shot at Imogen as soon as he entered the incident room.

"Julian's working flat out on the case, sir. He should have something for us soon."

Soon just wasn't fast enough. Lydia was running out of time.

"With a bit of luck there'll be a match on the database."

"We can only hope so. Keep at him. We need that result, and quick."

Lydia had been gone all day. The murdering bastard had her, was keeping her somewhere and, for all he knew, the poor woman was already dead. The more he thought about her, the angrier he got. It should never have happened. He slammed his fist on his desk, making Imogen jump. He was helpless, floundering around with nothing to go on.

"We're doing all we can, sir. And don't forget, she's a bright woman, very resourceful. If there's a way out, then she'll find it."

The DC was trying to be kind, but he knew the score. Lydia was in grave danger, and it was all his fault.

"I'll have another trawl through the records. I've now got access to the local adoption stuff. The powers that be didn't like it, but, as I told them, this is a murder inquiry. I'll find out who David Morpeth was fostered with. If they still live locally, then they may know his biological family."

That was a good idea. Imogen was shaping up to be a damn good detective. Imogen, Rocco and Ruth — they were all first class. With a bit of luck, Dodgy would emulate them, but Calladine couldn't help noticing that he was beginning to live up to his nickname.

"Where's Dodgy gone? Long's team will be back with the CCTV from Hopecross any time and I want him to help them look through it."

"He's gone out to do something for Ruth; back to the Hobfield, I think."

Calladine nodded. Just so long as he was doing something, and contributing to the case. There was no place on his team for a person who didn't pull their weight.

He needed to nip out himself. He still had to get Monika's present. He picked up the phone to ring her. He would stay at hers tonight. She'd said she'd cook. Otherwise he knew he wouldn't bother eating at all.

"Glad you rang, Tom. I was just about to contact you. Your mum's in hospital — Leesworth General. It's her legs again. She was doing okay, then this morning they were bad again. The doctor's been and he's sent her in. Her skin is so thin, it's breaking down and badly infected. They'll keep an eye on her for a couple of days, give her antibiotics and see how she goes."

"I'll go and see her now. I've got to check on Rocco anyway. Then I'll meet you at yours later. Is that okay?"

"Fine. I'll cook. See you soon, lover," she laughed and put the phone down. *Lover.* How was he going to deal with that one? And after what he'd done, should he even try? What had got into him lately, and why did poor Monika always have to get the rough end? But if he was honest with himself, he knew very well why. It could be summed up in two words — Lydia Holden. He was a fickle bastard.

He couldn't help it. He liked Lydia. Perhaps it was more than that, but could that happen so soon in a relationship? Quite probably, in his case. With him, these things had to simply run their course and then, with any luck, burn themselves out. He hoped so. As it was, he had her face in his head and her voice ringing in his ears. She'd got to him. One night in her bed and he was like a lovesick puppy.

And now she was out there, somewhere, and that lunatic was tormenting her — hurting her. He slammed the receiver down on his desk with a resounding crash. He had to find her. Sod his mother, sod Monika — Lydia had to come first.

"Ruth? Got a minute?"

"What's up, sir?"

"We're missing something — something fundamental. I just keep thinking that we're not seeing this for what it is."

"It's simple. It's murder, sir, that's what it is. He's a bloody head case who gets his rocks off by doing all that stuff."

"But why? Why the name *Handy Man* for example? What's the significance of that — any ideas?"

"No, but it must mean something to him. He's trying to tell us something, perhaps why he's doing this. For reasons we can only guess at, getting rid of Edwards, Hurst and Masheda in that way was important to him. Otherwise why not just shoot them? We know he has a gun. The name goes together with the handprints. And you're right, if we could work it out, then we'd have the answer and our man."

"I agree. I think they're the key to this entire thing. Have a look at the HOLMES database — see if there's anyone with similar form, or if anything like this has happened before. Also look again at the Morpeth death. Look at the detail and see if there's anything there."

* * *

Returning to her desk, Ruth found Jake Ireson's card and rang him.

"Sorry to disturb you at school. But can we meet? Possibly after classes?"

"Sure Ruth. Do you want to eat somewhere? Is this the date we spoke about?" He laughed.

"No, we'll have to leave that one for later, at the weekend. This is more in the nature of work, Jake. I want to ask you a few things and show you something. Can you come here to the station on your way home?"

"Surely. I'll be with you about four — that okay?"

"In the meantime, try and remember all you can about the bullying. I know that Edwards and Hurst were front runners, but what about a lad called Malcolm Masheda?"

"Yeah — he was involved too. There was one very nasty incident, as I recall."

"Okay, tell me later and anything else you can think of."

Ruth wanted to run the hand-print stuff past him and see if it had any relevance at all to what went on back then when David Morpeth had been killed.

* * *

"The bullets — they're a match! Imogen jumped up from her chair and grabbed the printout that had just come through.

She knocked on Calladine's door and thrust it into his hand. "You were right, sir! The bullets that killed Richard Pope and injured Cuba are from the same gun."

That was great news and no more than he had expected. Not that it would prove much in a court of law. The lawyers would simply argue that, given the nature of the Hobfield, the gun would have been sold on. Same gun did not mean same perpetrator. But Calladine believed differently.

"I got nothing from HOLMES." Ruth's voice filtered through the open door. "But I've asked Jake to come in later. He may recognise that." She nodded at the incident board.

One step forward, one step back. This case wasn't moving fast enough. There were still too many unanswered questions. He was frustrated that he couldn't do anything more to help poor Lydia. Lydia, Monika, his mother — each of them was getting to him in different ways, and he was tired. This bastard, whoever he was, was running him and his team ragged.

"Julian's coming in," Imogen said through the open door. "He needs to speak to you about something. Oh, and that bit of film — there was nothing much when I cleaned it up. Ice was fastened to what looked like a girder against a stone wall."

He hoped Julian would have something useful. He'd have to put off visiting his mother until he'd heard what the forensic scientist had to say.

"He really wants to help sort this, sir. You know what he's like — if the answer's in the forensic evidence somewhere, then Julian will find it."

Imogen wasn't wrong. What Julian had found was just what Calladine wanted to hear.

"There was no exact database match to the DNA we got from the saliva on the briefcase. But what we do have is a familial match."

That was what Calladine had thought. His instincts had been twitching since he'd heard the name earlier. "The Morpeth boy?"

Julian nodded.

He knew they'd have David Morpeth's DNA on record. This was looking more and more as if his brother, Michael, was their man.

"The saliva came from a very close relative of David Morpeth."

"His brother perhaps?"

"Very possibly — brother, father, uncle. So yes, it's safe to assume, as a hypothesis only at this time, that it came from his brother."

"In the absence of anything better, then, I will. Pin back your ears, team, and spread the word to uniform and Inspector Long's team. We are looking for Michael Morpeth. I want him bringing in as a matter of urgency. Find him, stop him and get the bastard in the cells. Ruth — do we have any idea what he looks like?"

"No, sir, all we know is that he is about thirty years of age."

"Imogen — keep at those records. You might turn up something more. We need to know who David Morpeth's foster carer was. His brother may have visited. They might be able to give us a description. Worth a try, don't you think?" Ruth nodded in response. "Also, we need more information about the Morpeth family. The elderly woman I saw today, for example. I want to know where she lives."

The incident room became a hive of activity. The new evidence spurred the team on. They were close, suddenly, after days of frustration and despair. Calladine felt renewed confidence that he might — just — get his man.

He went to report to DCI Jones, who was as dismissive as ever. It was obvious that he still thought this was down to drugs. Bloody fool.

Ruth knocked on the DCI's office. "Kelly Griggs is downstairs," she reported.

Chapter 21

Kelly Griggs sat in the tiny waiting room, rocking the baby in her arms.

"He's cranky," she said to the two detectives. "We've been on a train and then a taxi ride from Manchester Piccadilly, so he's shattered."

Ruth smiled at her and sat down at her side. "We're glad you've come in, Kelly. Would you like someone to push him around for a bit in his pram? Give you time to talk to us properly."

"Okay, but only inside. I want to hear him if he cries. Walk him up and down the corridor. He'll drop off within a few minutes."

Ruth nipped out and returned with a female PC in tow, who took hold of Jack, tucked him into his pram and wheeled him away.

"I've heard about Ice, but that's not why I've come. Donna told me he died — was killed — days ago. So that means it couldn't have been him who left me this." She set down a bag of cash on the bench beside her.

"That looks like a lot of money, Kelly."

"Nearly three thousand pounds, less what I've just spent on a couple of days away and some stuff I bought for Jack. You take it. I don't want it now, and it's got blood all over it."

"Tell me how you come to have this."

"It was left on my doorstep late on Monday night — or early Tuesday morning, I'm not sure. I thought Ice had left it, but now I know he couldn't have done."

"It does look like drugs money, though." Calladine picked up one of the rolls and examined it closely. "Given what we already know, it could well have been on Ice when he was taken."

"What happened to him?"

"We can't tell you everything, Kelly. Not yet." Ruth laid a comforting hand on the girl's arm.

"Ice, Gavin and Malcolm Masheda have all been murdered, we believe by the same person. We don't have much, but today we've made some real progress on the case." Calladine told her.

She paused. The girl looked washed out. The break hadn't done her much good then. She was very thin and pale, and wore her long, dark hair pulled tightly back in an austere ponytail which did her no favours. Not very flattering, but probably practical, with a demanding infant to attend to at all hours of the day and night.

"We do have one or two questions, if you feel up to answering them. You all went to school together. While you were there, did you know David Morpeth?"

Kelly nodded. "Everyone knew David. He was weird. But what's it got to do with him? That was years ago."

"He was killed. The death was deemed suspicious, and Ice was implicated," Calladine reminded her. "I don't know how or why, but I think David's death is somehow linked to what happened to Ice and the others."

"Well David can't do much, can he? Not from beyond the grave. Ice never said anything much about it. Neither he or Gavin would ever talk about what happened that day."

"Was it them? Did Ice push David down the stairs?"

Kelly shrugged. "I think Ice stuck his leg out and tripped him up. I heard Gavin joking about it once. But I don't think he meant for him to fall so hard or so far. Ice said nobody could prove anything and everyone had to keep their mouths shut. He didn't care. Ice was hard like that. As far as he was concerned David was expendable — nothing but a waste of space."

A real nice lad, even back then, Calladine thought bitterly. The incident with David might have happened a while ago, but if Calladine was right then his brother had certainly not forgotten. But why had he waited all this time to get revenge? It didn't make any sense.

"I know that Ice has always been pally with Gavin, but what I don't understand is Mash's part in all this. He wasn't even around when David was killed."

She looked at Calladine and shook her head. "The other stuff — the bullying; he was part of that. He was every bit as bad as Ice when it came to picking on David."

"So Ice, Gavin and Mash made David Morpeth's life a misery — is that what you're saying?"

"It was worse than that. They were cruel and vindictive. David was weird so he was a loner and he had nobody on his side. The whole school sided with Ice and his gang. They egged them on until things got completely out of hand."

"What do you mean, Kelly?"

She didn't answer.

Ruth had noticed something. "There's a note with the money. It's tied on the bag with a pink ribbon." Snapping on a pair of gloves, she picked it up '*You did a kind thing,*' it read.

'Do you know what this means? What particular kind thing is it referring to, Kelly? What was it you did that would make someone give you all this money?"

"I don't know. I've thought about it, of course I have. To give me three thousand pounds you'd think it would be something big, something I'd remember. But I don't."

Calladine didn't think she was lying. Why should she? And she'd brought the money in when she heard that Ice was dead. Kelly Griggs wanted to help them. She wasn't holding back.

Ruth looked at Calladine and nodded at the folder. "Should I, sir?"

Calladine stood up and sighed. What difference would it make? He looked at the young girl. She was strong enough to withstand seeing the images. He nodded back at Ruth.

"Kelly, I'm going to show you something," Ruth said, reaching for the folder. "But you mustn't tell anyone else what you see. Not yet. It might be needed as evidence in court, and we don't want the entire estate knowing what's going on and prejudicing the outcome. This is very important. Do you understand?"

Kelly nodded. She knew all about keeping her mouth shut.

"Does this mean anything to you, anything at all?" Ruth held up a photo of the red handprint and watched Kelly's eyes widen.

The image took Kelly right back to that day — that awful day, and what happened to David. "That's what they did to David, the three of them." She looked like she wanted to cry. "I don't know how I could forget something like that." She pushed a stray lock of hair back from her face. "Perhaps I just stuck it at the back of my mind because it was so wicked and it upset me. It was one of the worst things they did — apart from killing him, of course. But it happened ages before David fell down the stairs."

"Tell us, Kelly. Tell us what happened."

"They got him — David — the three of them. They had him in the caretaker's shed. They wanted to punish him for something — I can't remember what, but things got rough. They were hitting him, slapping him, and they made his mouth bleed. He was pushed against the shelves and a can of red paint got knocked over. Mash said he tried to clear it up and got it all over his hands. He started to daub it all over David. Ice and Gavin thought this was a right laugh and they joined in. They pinned David down and hand-printed his skin and his clothes. They made a right mess of him. It was in his hair, his eyes and everything. He was in a right state and bleeding from his mouth and his nose. I tried to help. When they'd gone I started to clean him up. I did my best but it was gloss paint — bright red gloss paint. It looked just like fresh blood. In the end I couldn't tell what was what. I had no choice; I had to take him home."

"To his foster parents?"

"No. They'd have gone mad. What she was doing fostering kids I don't know, because she'd no patience at all. There was no kindness in her."

"Who was that, Kelly?"

"Joyce Pope. She was a dreadful woman. She had David scared half to death. She had his brother too, but he wised up and got out. David was too young so he couldn't take him with him."

Ruth and Calladine looked at each other.

Was that why Richard Pope had been killed? Calladine wondered. Was it possible that Morpeth had a new identity and Pope could have jeopardised it? He'd certainly have recognised him, he'd have seen him often enough when his mother had fostered David. Michael Morpeth must have worried that Richard would have given the game away. But whom was he masquerading as?

"Kelly, if David's brother, Michael, came back to Leesdon would you know him, could you pick him out from a current photo?"

"Michael was into punk back then. He had his hair dyed jet black and half of it shaved off. His face was often covered in odd makeup. He didn't hang out with the local kids and he was a right weirdo. So, no I might not, particularly if he's smartened up, got a regular hairstyle.

171

That meant that Michael Morpeth could be living among them. And Kelly was right — he would be an older, toned-down version of the lad everyone recalled from back then. He could pass unnoticed but not to Richard Pope.

"On that day I took him to Michael," Kelly continued. "He was creepy, but I knew he'd sort him out. David would do anything for Michael and vice versa. David was odd, like I said, but Michael was worse. David wasn't always a good lad, but Michael was evil. He used to make me shudder, but he was always okay with David."

There was a sudden knock on the door. It was Imogen. She peeped in and gestured towards Calladine.

"The emails and stuff that were sent to Lydia Holden. They were sent from the IT suite at the community centre and they have cameras in there."

Ruth smiled. "Thanks, Imogen."

"What was Michael like? I've seen photos of David and he was small for his age but overweight."

"He was fat, you mean. That was half the problem, that and his autism. Michael and David were very different. Michael was tall, wiry, with dark, longish hair which he had done in a punky style."

"Do you know where he went when he left the Pope's?"

"At first he went back to his mother. She was a drunk — a hopeless woman. After that — after she killed herself — I don't know what he did. I wasn't really bothered, to be honest. He wasn't talked about much. No one liked him."

"Thank you, Kelly. I'll get you a lift home. We may need to talk to you again, so no more disappearing — okay?"

Kelly nodded and rose wearily off the bench.

"Ice gave me a hard time, but I wouldn't want him dead. You will get whoever did this, won't you?"

Calladine nodded. He was beginning to believe now that he really would.

"The emails were sent from the community centre. Not very clever." Ruth pointed out.

"Perhaps he had no choice," Calladine mused. "Whoever we are looking for, Michael Morpeth or not, has a place — perhaps in the wilds, up near the moors. What chance they have broadband up there?"

"We'd better go take a look. They keep logs and have good security. With any luck we may get a look at our man. We could certainly do with that particular piece of the puzzle."

Chapter 22

He could hear Lydia begin to sob as he opened the cellar door.

"Please . . . don't do this. I won't tell anyone. It can be our secret." She called out to him, her voice faltering with emotion.

He laughed. Secret or not — he didn't care. It was time for him to be selfish, enjoy a little *me time*. The others, the young men, had been boring compared to her. All that chopping, coming up with inventive ways to dispatch them. Mash had been good though. His disembowelment had been a treat to watch. The look on the youth's face when he'd realised the full implications. Thoughts of the horror of waiting in so much agony for the end to come had brought on that feeling again, the one he enjoyed so much.

But she was different. Lydia Holden was beautiful, with a lovely female body to lavish his attentions on. He'd keep her for a while and have some fun. All his relationships with women, the few there'd been, had ended in tatters. This time he'd call the shots. She was in no position to complain or to refuse him. He felt the excitement rise. There were a lot of things he wanted to try on that sweet body of hers. It'd be good practice for when he made a play for Kelly.

Kelly had always been the one he wanted. Even back in school, he'd liked her. But she'd gone and wasted her time on that idiot, Ice. Why do women do that? He'd never understand. Kelly and Ice. Now Lydia and that stupid detective — why didn't they see? He was all they needed.

These thoughts tormented him and he felt the anger rise. "Bitch. Stupid bitch. You deserve everything you get. No one is coming for you, no one knows where you are." He leaned over her, his breathing heavy, his face florid with rage. He had to make her see — she had to be taught a lesson.

Lydia screamed. He heard the noise she made echo in the dark, bleak space. Did she not realise how hopeless it was? That there was nothing she could do. She'd die here in agony and no one would ever know. His beautiful reporter would die realising that she'd made a huge mistake. He was the one she should have chosen and not that stupid detective.

Was he still looking? Of course he was, the detective was like a dog with a bone. But he wouldn't find her. He'd fret and he'd search, he'd work his team into a frazzle but it would do no good. He was far too clever for him. He'd outwitted the detective inspector at every turn, he realised proudly. And now he could claim the prize.

She was whimpering, he hated that. He slapped her thigh. "Stop it! Shut the fuck up!"

"I . . . I can't help it," she mumbled.

"Shut up! You're starting to get on my nerves. Why are you like this, why don't you understand that this is where you belong — here with me?"

He could see her shivering and even hear her teeth chattering with cold.

"Shut it, bitch! You're making too much noise. I can't hear." He was straining to listen to something else.

"Did you hear that?"

* * *

Lydia had reached the end of her endurance. She couldn't take anymore and her heart was hammering so fast she couldn't hear anything either. She was too traumatised to even listen at first. What was he talking about? *Did you hear that?* he'd asked. Why — had someone come to the house? Had he heard knocking on the door? She tried to pull herself together, turning her head wildly from side to side and inhaling deeply, preparing to scream for all she was worth.

Her body seemed to wake up and ready itself. Adrenaline, she reasoned. If there was someone here, then she had to make sure they heard her. Then she saw it. There was a series of small red lights flashing on a shelf across the room. She tried harder to listen. There came a series of low moans, followed by a loud thud. It was a baby monitor. The bastard had a baby monitor down here. Why? —And more to the point, who did he have upstairs? Surely not an infant; no one would leave a child in his care.

Then in the blink of an eye he was gone. Lydia heard a door open followed by the sound of his footsteps as he ran up a staircase. Something had happened; something that bothered him enough to make him run like that. He'd heard something on the monitor and had gone to check it out. But what had he heard? She turned her head. Yes, this time he'd left the door open. If she could pull hard enough, get free then she'd make a run for it. But it was hopeless. She was bound with chains attached to manacles fixed to the bench.

"Fucking, bastard maniac!" she shrieked into the gloom. "Get down here and let me go, you fucking lunatic!"

Then he was back. "She's fallen," his voice quivered. "She's up there on the floor, and she's not moving at all. What shall I do?"

"Who's fallen? Who the hell are you talking about?"

"None of your business. Forget it." And he left the room again.

Lydia was mystified. Whatever was going on had him rattled. She had to think. This was a situation she should be ready to exploit.

He came back.

"I think she's seriously hurt. I can't stand to see her like that. She looks so small, and there's blood . . ." There was real emotion — fear — in the words.

Gone was the cold, calculated killer, and in his place was a man with a quaking voice, unsure of what to do next. She had to think. This sudden change of mood was a chance not to be missed. Perhaps she should offer to help him. If she played things right, it could be her chance to escape.

"Is she breathing?" Lydia spoke gently, trying to sound as concerned as she could.

"How should I know?" He held his head in his hands and made a sort of howling noise that reverberated around the cellar. "It's all my fault. No it's not." The tone of his voice had changed again. "It's hers. She's a stupid old woman. Why can't she do as she's told? I told her not to move, but she doesn't understand; she gets confused. I said I'd get the supper and she didn't have to bother. I wish she'd listen to me!" His voice rose to a whine.

"Do you want me to help?" Lydia posed the question as calmly as she could. "I think you do. I think you need someone to look at her; someone who can judge what's going on." She tried to sound matter of fact. He must believe that she could really make a difference. "I have first-aid training, you know. I can do CPR and everything. Has she knocked her head?"

"I don't know. Should I check?"

"That's a good idea. Yes, go and check and then we can work out what to do."

He disappeared again. This was surreal. He'd become a different entity. He was dithering, almost pliable. She'd never get a better chance. If he would only untie her, then she might still have a chance.

Now he was actually crying. "There's a lot of blood. All over her head, running down her face, and she still hasn't got up."

Lydia put more urgency into her words, "She obviously needs help. If we don't act straight away, then a bang on the head could be very dangerous indeed. We don't want anything awful to happen to her, do we? Because we know who everyone will blame? They'd say it was our fault, but we can put them right, can't we? We can tell them what we did for her. How brave we both were."

"First-aid training? You're not just saying that to fool me into letting you go? Because if you don't help her I'll be very angry and it'll be worse for you."

"No, no, of course not. I can see that this is serious and I wouldn't lie about something like that. At one time I almost became a nurse," she lied. "I can help, I know I can, and you know this is the right thing to do, don't you? Think how terrible it would be if she died."

He let out a high-pitched quivering scream and went to her side again. "I can't lose her. I need her to live. She's all I've got left of the old life."

He was pulling at the chains. She'd done it — he was releasing her. Lydia felt a surge of relief as she was finally able to sit up and rub some life back into her limbs. So far so good.

"Where is she? Upstairs?"

"We'll go slow. You first, and she's in the kitchen. Top of the stairs, turn right."

"Do you think I could have a blanket or a robe? I'm naked and cold and you're embarrassing me, staring like that."

He looked her up and down, as if seeing her for the first time, and threw her a dirty old sheet, which Lydia promptly wrapped around her.

"Up you go. One false move and you're history, bitch. Understand?"

Lydia nodded. She understood only too well. This would be her only chance. Whatever she did now had to be final. This maniac would kill her if she failed.

Upstairs, she could see that the building was old; a largish house or even a farm. The walls were made of local stone, like the mill she lived in. The furniture was old — dark wood, and covered in dust and junk. No one had cleaned for a long time. The curtains were drawn tightly closed, but the fabric was thin. There were no street lights outside, but she could just make out the light from the full moon in the night sky. The countryside then — perhaps up in the Pennines somewhere, above Leesworth.

"Why did you leave her so near to the fire? Her arm has been lying across the grate and it's badly burned."

The elderly woman was lying unconscious on the kitchen floor. She looked terribly frail, almost emaciated. There was a large gash across her right temple, which was still pouring blood. From the way she lay, it looked as though she'd fallen from her chair.

"I'll need a clean towel. In fact, fetch two, one for her head and one to soothe this arm."

He went to a drawer in the side of a large oak table and produced two thick tea towels.

"I want you to keep this one pressed hard against the wound on her head. We need to stop the bleeding."

He was dithering again. He didn't seem to want to touch the woman. "Go on. Press it hard. I need to soak this one in cold water for her arm."

Amazingly, he did as she told him without argument. He was kneeling beside the woman, rocking back and forth on his knees and whispering to her.

"Who is she?" Lydia let the water run until it flowed icy.

"My grandmother. We can't let her die. I need her." And now he was pleading with her; only minutes ago, he'd been planning to kill her.

"Don't worry, she'll be okay. Are you going to call for an ambulance?"

"No! No. I don't want anyone coming here." He was yelling again. "I know your game, bitch. You think I'm stupid. Well I'm not, so forget it."

The old woman on the floor really did need proper help; she was in a bad way. Lydia looked around, her eyes frantically searching for something — a weapon to hit him with. It had to be hard and it had to be heavy. She'd only get one chance.

"This is a kind thing you're doing. I won't forget that you helped me — and her. I never forget things like that. Ask Kelly." His moods veered crazily, and Lydia knew she needed to get out of here before he became manic again.

"But it doesn't change anything. It can't. You know too much about me. You'll tell others — that inspector of yours, and he'll lock me up. I can't have that. I can't let that happen."

"Is she coming round yet?" Lydia pointedly ignored this comment.

"No, she isn't doing anything. She's not moving and the bleeding won't stop."

"Put your head on her chest. Check if her breathing's regular."

He bent down low with his back to her. This was it. She wouldn't get a better opportunity. By the fire there were a number of heavy objects, including a heavy cast-iron poker.

Lydia darted to the side and grabbed it. It was now or never. Swinging it high she sprang forward and brought it crashing down across the back of his head.

She saw the blood spurt. She saw him turn momentarily with a look of utter shock on his face. Then she watched as he fell onto his back — unconscious.

Lydia had no time to dwell on what she'd done or to think about the old woman. She scuttled around the kitchen looking for something to tie his hands with. She found a leather belt and fastened it around his wrists as tightly as she could. She used the tieback from the curtains to bind his ankles. Now she needed to find a phone.

Despite rendering him helpless, she was still very nervous about leaving him in the kitchen; he might wake up and get out. But she had no choice. She had to get help, and she didn't have it in her to kill him in cold blood, despite what he'd done to her. She made a quick search of the house. She searched the cluttered furniture in the sitting room, until finally she found her things — most importantly, her mobile phone. Now she could call for help and get the hell out of here.

Chapter 23

"I want a word with the IT technician and whoever looks after your security, please." Calladine flashed his warrant card at the woman sitting at the community centre desk.

"Craig Barker looks after the IT suite." She pressed a button on the intercom.

"Craig to main desk!" Her voice rang out across the complex.

Craig Barker was young and looked very much like all the other youths who used the computers here.

"Yeah? Want a machine? Do you have login details?"

Calladine shook his head. "No, son, we don't want to use anything. We want to ask you some questions. I'm DI Calladine and this is DS Ruth Bayliss."

The young man shrugged and deposited a piece of well-chewed gum in the rubbish bin.

"Fire away."

"A couple of emails were sent from here earlier on this week. I have the headers. Are you able to show me which machine was used and tell me who used it on those days?"

Craig looked at the paperwork. "Yeah, follow me . . . I keep a log: machine number; IP addresses. Just give me a minute."

Calladine looked at Ruth and raised his eyebrows. So far, so good.

"Yep, here we are. PC number ten. I've got the user down here as a *Mikey*. He stayed for thirty five minutes then left."

"Do you have any CCTV?"

"Should have. Want to look?"

Calladine and Ruth followed Craig to a side room and watched as he rummaged through a number of CDs.

"This should be the one."

They watched a number of customers come and go over the afternoon. They were mostly lads from the estate, and no one was making any attempt to hide their identity. Then they saw him.

He had on the same hooded top as he'd been wearing when he took Lydia. He spoke to the girl on the IT reception desk for a few moments, signed the log book and slipped onto a chair in front of a computer. He was at it again, making sure that his back faced the camera at all times. Another rear view — great!

"Is there any way we can get to see his face?"

Craig grinned. He got himself comfortable at the keyboard, as if waiting for something. Then, just at the very moment their man turned his machine off, he froze the screen. For a second or two the reflection shone back at them. He was caught in his own blank monitor. Craig zoomed in, and it was just possible to see him face on.

Calladine and Ruth both craned forward and then looked at each other in disbelief.

"No!" Ruth gasped. "I don't believe it. That can't be right. There must be some mistake. This must have been when he was checking something for us. That's got to be it, hasn't it, sir?"

But Calladine knew it was no mistake. His clothes gave him away. This was the man who'd taken Lydia. There was no way round this, upsetting as it was going to be for all of them. But there was no getting away from the raw facts. He'd suspected all along that Michael Morpeth was one step ahead; that he was getting information he shouldn't have had access to. Morpeth knew exactly how to operate, and now Calladine knew why. Ignoring Ruth's cries, he got on his phone again and spoke to Imogen.

"Imogen, has Dodgy come back in yet?"

"No, guv, he's got a problem at home. He rang in earlier. Apparently his Granny is ill and he's had to go and see to her."

"Do you know where she lives?"

"Yep, she lives at Hobrise Farm. Leaving Hopecross, it's on the road towards the West Yorkshire border. For the last few weeks Dodgy's been staying with her, that's how I know."

A spot that was both isolated and difficult to find. Perfect.

Calladine asked to be put through to DCI Jones.

"Sir, the man we want is Michael Morpeth, Hobrise Farm, on the border road. He's kidnapped Lydia Holden and God knows who else, so we need a full back-up team up there, and an ambulance. Make sure someone's armed as well."

This time Jones didn't quibble about the costs. "There is something else, sir, and it isn't good. Michael Morpeth has been using an alias, and we know him."

There was a silence.

"We know him as Michael Dodgson, sir, Dodgy. Our Dodgy."

Ruth folded her arms and started to pace the floor. She couldn't believe — she wouldn't believe it. Something had to be wrong. She looked again at the frozen image on the screen and shook her head.

"We should get going." Calladine made for the door.

"He's been planning this for years, hasn't he? He's waited all this time to get back at Ice and the others because of what they did to his brother. He even changed his surname just to fool us. But Kelly said he was dark — dark haired, don't you remember? Dodgy is blonde."

"Hair's easily dyed, Ruth," he muttered irritably. He averted his eyes from Ruth's gaze. He was upset. He felt severely let down. This was one of his own.

"Are we going with this, sir?" Ruth was floundering, looking for guidance. "Is it even possible? Do we really think that . . . do you think that Dodgy's capable of doing all those things?"

Calladine had suspected nothing. Dodgy had been shaping up to be a good cop. So why go and ruin everything like this? Calladine and Ruth walked outside into the cold evening air. He supposed the question he should be asking was why had Dodgy put himself through all the training to become a detective in the first place, if all he wanted was to commit murder? But then wasn't that the perfect training ground?

His phone rang; he was half expecting it to be Imogen But it wasn't. It was Lydia.

* * *

"Tom! I've knocked him out, but he might come round, and if he does he'll kill me! You need to come. I need help at once."

His relief at hearing her voice was almost overwhelming. He could hardly believe he was actually talking to her. He'd half expected never to see or hear her again. But she'd made it. Imogen had been right to call her resourceful.

"Calm down. I know what's happened, and I know where you are. There's police and an ambulance on the way. Get outside right away; hide somewhere and don't make yourself known until you see the lights. The officers will be armed. So don't worry, they'll get him."

"My signal's breaking up . . ." She tapped the phone against the wall in frustration. But it was no use — Tom had gone. At least help was on its way, but how long would she have to wait?

The front door was locked and there was no key. She had no choice but to go out the back door. Lydia tiptoed back through the kitchen and past the two prone bodies. It was a nightmare, like something from a cheap horror movie. He groaned and moved his legs, making her jump. Then his eyelids fluttered open — just for a second — but it frightened the life out of her. He couldn't come round yet, he just couldn't. She was terrified and shaking again. Lydia knew she had no choice — it was either him or her. She grabbed the poker that was still lying on the floor where she'd left it. She aimed at his head, closed her eyes and gave him a second whack. The poker struck his head with an awful clunk of bone and iron. It did the trick, he was out cold again.

The back door was bolted top and bottom. But the bolts were stiff and wouldn't give. She cried out with frustration and tried again, using all her strength, but she was all fingers and thumbs. She needed to calm down; try again, and slowly this time . . . Finally she eased them open and ran full pelt into the back garden.

The moon was hazy, as though covered in gauze. There were no houses nearby that she could run to, no street lights. In fact, she couldn't even see a road — just a dirt track leading up to the house. What to do? Where to go? She had to find somewhere; for she believed absolutely that if he came round and got free, he'd find her, no matter what she did. She hunkered down behind a huge oak tree, shivering with fear and cold, praying for help to arrive soon.

Chapter 24

The Pennine road that led over the tops into West Yorkshire was narrow and dark, but Ruth and Calladine were racing. Then his phone rang.

"They've got her, sir, she's safe." Imogen was barely able to hide her excitement. The mobile was on loudspeaker, and both detectives heard the good news. "She's in the ambulance on her way to the General."

"Handy Man — Michael Morpeth?" He didn't mention Dodgy's name. He wanted to tell his team personally.

"He's been arrested by uniform. He's on his way to the General too. Lydia gave him quite a whack, and he's still groggy."

He smiled — good girl. "Okay — we'll turn around and meet them there. Thanks, Imogen."

"By the way, sir, I don't know how important it is now but the woman who lives at the farm — is Annie Dodgson. She's Dodgy's granny — did you know that, sir?"

Calladine merely grunted a reply. So much for wanting to do this gently.

"Well Julian's people are all over that place and he rang to say she's on all those pills you were looking for — every last one of them."

That didn't surprise him. The pieces were all falling the right way up at last. What was the betting that Dodgy had changed his name from Morpeth to Dodgson when he went to live with his granny? New name, new identity, and then a career that would teach him all the skills he'd need to avoid detection. So why had he craved the publicity so much? What was that all about? "We'll make for the General," he told Ruth. "My mum, Lydia and our man, plus Rocco — we can go see them all."

The fact that Lydia had been found had lightened his mood but he still had no idea how bad things were. Or what he was going to tell the team. How to deal with the fact that one of your own was so evil; committing murder right under their very eyes?

First, he pulled over to swap places with Ruth. "Do you mind driving us back? I'm bushed. I'm sorry, we're going to be late again and you've missed your date with Jake. Will he understand?"

"He'll have to if he wants to keep on seeing me." She grinned.

"I can't wait to get home tonight. A couple of beers and a good long lie in tomorrow."

"It's Monika's birthday tomorrow. Aren't you supposed to be staying with her tonight?"

"Damn! I forgot and I didn't make the Antiques Centre either. D'you reckon she'll understand?"

"No! She'll be bloody annoyed — and with every right. You're a disgrace, Tom Calladine, and well you know it."

"So what am I going to do?"

Ruth delved into her handbag and produced a rectangular velvet box and a birthday card.

"Here, give her this. Check it out and then I'll wrap it while you write the card."

The necklace was perfect. A string of turquoise stones set in silver.

"And you owe me fifty quid. I won't charge you anything for going."

"You're a real mate, Ruth Bayliss. I won't forget this, I promise. I'll drop this off later on my way home. But between now and then you have to help me come up with an excuse not to stay the night."

"No way — she's my friend, remember? I've saved your bacon with the present, and after that you're on your own."

"You'd be doing me an enormous favour . . . You do work on my team, so you need to keep me sweet."

"I've done enough with the present. I won't lie to her for you, so don't ask me again." And Ruth stuck her nose in the air.

* * *

"Who first?" They were pacing the hospital corridor yet again.

"You'd better go see Lydia, and I'll check on Rocco. Then we'll both see our man."

Lydia Holden was sitting in a cubicle in the Emergency Department. She was wearing a hospital gown. The sheet she'd arrived in had been bagged for forensics. A sober thought and one that filled Calladine with dread. What had the bastard done to her?

It was such a relief to see her alive and well. He flung his arms around her, and she nestled into his chest. He hardly dared ask. She looked okay — a little mud on her legs and arms, but what had Morpeth done to her? He looked into her eyes and saw the tears welling.

"Did he . . . did he hurt you?"

She lowered her eyes and shook her head. "It was awful, Tom. I thought I was going to die in the most dreadful way." The tears were now rolling down her cheeks. "He touched me, he would have done more, raped me but the old lady saved my bacon." She looked up into his face, hers tired and worn. "It was close, too close. If she hadn't fallen I'd be dead. He's a bloody maniac and you know him, you all know him."

"Yes I realise that now. But he was clever, until today he ran us ragged."

"You'll have to up your game, detective," she replied, her tone a little lighter.

"Are they keeping you in?"

"I don't want to stay. They've suggested counselling, but I'll see." She wiped her eyes. "That man's an animal. That accident the old lady had, saved my life. I was lucky, Tom, but it was far too close and it'll take a while before I'm back to normal. The experience is going to give me nightmares for months, I know it is."

"We have him now, so you're safe. He can't hurt you or anyone else. You have to try and relax. But you still can't print anything — not yet. You're going to have to wait until after the trial, Lydia."

"Do you really think that's all that bothers me," she retorted wriggling away from him. "I've been kidnapped, strapped naked to a bench and molested by a bloody lunatic. Do you really think I want to write about that?"

Yet again he'd proved he was first class at putting his foot in it. Calladine took her hand gently. "Sorry, I'm beat and my brains not in gear. I'll help, you can stay with me, or I'll stay with you. I'll take care of you. You don't have to worry," he assured her.

"Just as long as you don't expect too much for a while. I know I come across as one hard-faced, feisty female but this has shaken me up. I don't recognise the person in here, Tom," she said tapping her head.

"If you want to go home now, then I can take you," he offered. There was no way he could spend the night with Monika, not now.

"I'm going to have to leave you for a few minutes, that's all. I've got my mother and a colleague in here too. I'll take a statement tomorrow. You can get it all out. I'll be your sounding board."

He hugged her and then left to find his mother. What was happening to him? Lydia Holden had got to him in a way he didn't recognise. She'd been hurt and he wanted to protect her. It was a feeling he'd not had about anything or anyone for quite a while.

His phone rang. It was Imogen again.

"Sir, he had Mash at the farm. He's dead I'm afraid, and Doctor Hoyle's lot have taken him. Uniform will tell his mum shortly, but not the detail; that's too ghastly. Julian says to tell you he's taken a whole load of tools from the cellar. He's going to test them against the slivers of metal found on the other bodies."

Everything falling into place then. That was a relief. There'd be no chance of him wriggling off the hook in court.

* * *

Freda Calladine was very poorly. She was in a side room of a medical ward. She was sleeping, struggling for each breath. He'd been told it was her legs, so why was she so ill? There was a young woman sitting beside her, someone he'd not seen before. Calladine said hello, presuming she was from the home.

"How's she doing?"

"They say she has a bad chest infection. The antibiotics aren't working properly, and they seem a bit dubious about the outcome, to be honest."

This was all he needed. "No one rang me," he said lamely. Not that he could have done much, given the pace of today. "Is Monika coming in?"

"Who?"

"Oh, I'm sorry, I thought you were from the home, here to keep an eye on her."

"No, I'm not, but I'm happy to stay with her for a bit if you're busy."

If she wasn't from the home, and she certainly wasn't dressed like a nurse, who was she?

"Are you some sort of volunteer visitor?"

She laughed at this and shook her head.

"You're her son, aren't you?"

Calladine nodded.

"I thought you might be. You are exactly as Freda described." She laughed. "This is going to come as a bit of a shock," she paused, "We've not met before, and that's not your fault or mine. I'm here because Freda is family: she's my granny."

He wondered at first if he'd heard her right. How could that be? In order for that to be so, he'd have to have a *daughter*!

"I'm not making myself very clear," she apologised. "I should have said straight away. I was hoping to do this differently but Granny being so ill put paid to that. I'm sorry, but I don't know how to put this." She looked at the inspector and then got to her feet and held out her hand.

"I'm Zoe — Zoe Calladine."

He blinked. *Zoe Calladine?* More confusion, and after the day he'd just had, he wasn't up to working it out.

"I'm Rachael's daughter. Rachael Calladine — your ex-wife."

Now he really was confused. Rachael had had a child but why keep his name?

"I'm still not making myself very clear, am I?" She paused, "This is going to come as a huge surprise, but you're my father."

Calladine blinked then stared at her. Was this some sort of wind-up? Who was this girl and why spin him a tale like this?

"I'm afraid Mum wasn't altogether honest with you all those years ago. She kept me to herself. When she went off to Bristol she was a few weeks pregnant. When I was born, she'd begun a new life so she never told you."

Now that did sound like Rachael. He'd listened to his mother's ramblings all week, but he'd not taken her seriously. As far as he knew Rachael and he had never had a child. No, of that he was certain. It hadn't been that bad a day!

"My mum was pregnant when you split up," Zoe explained again, seeing the confusion on his face. "She had no idea at the time you separated, and when she found out, she had a new life and didn't want the complication of having you involved. Not my words — hers," Zoe insisted. "She only told me the truth recently."

"Why on earth didn't she tell me? I don't understand . . . I could have helped. I could have supported you both."

"She didn't want that. She always said that it had to be a clean break. So, baby or not, she didn't want you to know. She told me about the break-up; you were never a secret. In fact there was a photo of you kept on the sideboard at home. It's just that she lied; she told me that you'd had an affair with another woman and you didn't want her or me. She also told me that you weren't interested in getting to know me."

"That's certainly not true. There was never another woman, not then. It was the job. I'm sorry, Zoe." He shook his head. "This is a huge shock. I'd no idea, not even a suspicion. If I'd known about you, I'd have been there straight away. This is a lot to take in," he said, rubbing his aching head. "How could she do this? Keep you secret all this time?"

Was she telling him the truth? Was this young woman really who she said she was. But if she wasn't, why lie — what could she possibly hope to gain?

Zoe smiled and sat down again. "It doesn't surprise me. She was like that. She cut all ties with you and with this place. She never came back, not once. My mum left, and that was that. She got on with things and she raised me. She studied and got a good job. She did very well. I'm proud of her."

"Has she come with you? What does she think of you coming here and making yourself known to me finally?"

"She wouldn't approve, but it doesn't matter because she'll never know now."

The words didn't sink in — it was all too much and his brain was reeling. First Lydia, now this. Add to the mix a bent cop, his sick mother, plus the Monika problem, and it'd been one helluva day.

"Shouldn't you phone her or something?"

"I can't. You see my mum — Rachael — died three months ago."

Calladine sank onto the edge of his mother's bed. Rachael dead. For heaven's sake, she was the same age as he was. He felt as if someone had just kicked him in the guts. He might not have seen her in years, but they had been married, been in love, at one time.

"Cancer. She had all the treatment, but it came back. There was nothing else they could do in the end."

"I am so sorry." He felt like weeping. She had been a big part of his life back then. Now he realised that she'd played an even bigger part than he'd known. She'd given him a daughter.

"I have no one in Bristol; a few friends but no family. So here I am." She smiled. "Mum finally told me the truth about you, so I thought I'd come and seek you out. I found granny first and was building up the courage to meet you."

"You shouldn't worry about me, Zoe, I'm a pussycat. Where are you staying?"

"At a pub on Leesdon High Street."

"The Wheatsheaf?"

She nodded.

"I live just off the High Street." He took one of his personal cards out of his wallet. "I've got two spare bedrooms, so why not come and stay with me?"

"Well . . . you might be my biological father, but I don't know you."

"I'm OK, believe me," he said wearily. "I'm a boring old fart of a detective inspector with the local police. I work a lot and I apprehend thieves and murderers. What else is there to know?"

She smiled. "Okay — perhaps in time, but for now I'll stay put. I'm going to sit with Granny for a while tonight, anyway. She really isn't well and the doctor said she wasn't responding to the medication."

Calladine bent over and looked at his aged mother. She was struggling for every breath. That wasn't good.

"I'll meet up with you tomorrow," Zoe suggested. "We can talk and get to know each other a bit better."

"Okay — if that's what you want."

A daughter. He liked the idea very much. She seemed nice, and she looked a lot like Rachael too. If things weren't so bloody grim he might even crack a smile.

It was his mother that was going to be the problem now. She looked ghastly — so pale and haggard. He patted her hand. He'd have to go. He had to find out where Ruth was, and see what had happened to their man. God. What was he going to tell the team? How was he going to explain that Dodgy was *Handy Man* — the murdering bastard they'd been searching for all week?

Ruth walked towards him along the corridor.

"He's sedated, sir. That was some bang on the head Lydia gave him. Anyway, we can't do anything tonight. If he's well enough, he'll be transferred to the cells tomorrow. We can speak to him then."

"Which room?"

"End of the corridor. There's a uniform with him."

Calladine strode down and knocked on the door. A uniformed constable opened it, and the inspector flashed his warrant card. He wanted to see him, to look at him. What for, he couldn't fathom. But seeing the truth behind the façade that had been Dodgy might help him to make sense of it.

The young man was hardly moving. He looked so still, so peaceful. He looked like Dodgy; young and vulnerable. Calladine had to remind himself who he really was.

"Time to go, sir." Ruth stuck her head around the door.

"That suits me. I could do with getting home but I'm needed here."

"Not coming to the pub for a celebratory drink? End of case, successful collar?"

"I can't. There's Lydia and it appears that I have a daughter."

"A daughter?" Ruth's eyes widened in surprise. "How did that happen — and who with?'

"With Rachael of course; my ex-wife. All those years ago when she left me, she was pregnant."

"Is she here? Your daughter, I mean."

"Yes. She's here tonight, visiting mum. We're going to talk tomorrow, then she might even agree to come and stay with me for a while."

"Well congratulations, Tom. I'm happy for you."

"It's about the only thing I've got to smile about right now," he admitted. "She's called Zoe, and she's lovely."

"Rocco's doing okay. He'll be out in a few days. Lydia?"

"She's in a bad way — mentally — I think. The bastard kept her tied up naked. She's traumatised, but she's a hard nut and she'll eventually bounce back."

"I'm going to get off then, sir. See you tomorrow at the nick."

A quick wave and she was gone. Calladine couldn't stay at Monika's now. He retrieved the present from his overcoat pocket — he'd drop it off at the care home and apologise. He had the perfect excuse for his absence. There was no way he could leave Lydia alone while she was still so traumatised. He wouldn't use that as his excuse to Monika though — he'd use his mother's condition.

He needed a quick breather before returning to Lydia. He inhaled the fresh night air and looked up at the sky. It was clear now and the moon was full and bright.

Tomorrow would be cold. But then tomorrow was another day.

THE END

Thank you for reading this book. If you enjoyed it please leave feedback on Amazon, and if there is anything we missed or you have a question about then please get in touch. The author and publishing team appreciate your feedback and time reading this book.

Our email is jasper@joffebooks.com

www.joffebooks.com

ALSO BY HELEN DURRANT

CALLADINE & BAYLISS MYSTERIES
DEAD WRONG
DEAD SILENT
DEAD LIST
DEAD LOST

DI GRECO
DARK MURDER

Made in the USA
Middletown, DE
29 August 2017